"About Last Night—"

Elyssa began unsteadily.

Alex pivoted to face her with the feral grace of a predator. "No," he said harshly. "We'll talk about last night...and this morning...in a few minutes. First we're going to talk about what happened between us six years and seven months ago on a Caribbean island called Corazon."

"Y-you?" she whispered, barely able to get the word out.

"Yes, me," he affirmed, taking his hands out of his pockets. He was holding a thin black billfold. She watched him flip it open and extract a tattered photograph. "Me and you."

He held out the snapshot. After a few moments, she took it from him and stared down at a token of the past she thought had been lost to her forever.

What she saw in the water-stained photograph was a man and a woman gazing deeply into each other's eyes.

The man was Alexander Moran.

The woman was...herself.

Dear Reader:

Happy New Year! 1991 is going to be a terrific year at Silhouette Desire. We've got some wonderful things planned, starting with another of those enticing, irresistible, tantalizing men. Yes, *Man of the Month* will continue through 1991!

Man of the Month kicks off with *Nelson's Brand* by Diana Palmer. If you remember, Diana Palmer launched *Man of the Month* in 1989 with her fabulous book, *Reluctant Father*. I'm happy to say that *Nelson's Brand* is another winner—it's sensuous, highly charged and the hero, Gene Nelson, is a man you'll never forget.

But January is not only *Man of the Month*. This month, look out for additional love stories, starting with the delightful *Four Dollars and Fifty-One Cents* by Lass Small. And no, I'm not going to tell you what the title means—you'll have to read the book! There's also another great story by Carole Buck, *Paradise Remembered,* a sexy adventure by Jean Barrett, *Heat,* and a real charmer from Cathie Linz, *Handyman.* You'll also notice a new name, Ryanne Corey. But I'm sure you'll want to know that she's already written a number of fine romances as Courtney Ryan. Believe me, *The Valentine Street Hustle* is a winner!

As for February... well, I can't resist giving you a peek into next month. Get ready for *Outlaw* by Elizabeth Lowell! Not only is this a *Man of the Month*, it's also another powerful WESTERN LOVERS series.

You know, I could go on and on... but I'll restrain myself right now. Still, I will say that 1991 is going to be filled with wonderful things from Silhouette Desire. January is just the beginning!

All the best,
Lucia Macro
Senior Editor

CAROLE BUCK

PARADISE REMEMBERED

SILHOUETTE *Desire*®

Published by Silhouette Books New York

America's Publisher of Contemporary Romance

SILHOUETTE BOOKS
300 East 42nd St., New York, N.Y. 10017

PARADISE REMEMBERED

ISBN: 0-373-05614-1

First Silhouette Books printing January 1991

Printed in the U.S.A.

Books by Carole Buck

Silhouette Desire

Time Enough for Love #565
Paradise Remembered #614

Silhouette Romance

Make-believe Marriage #752

CAROLE BUCK

is a television news writer and movie reviewer who lives in Atlanta. She is single. Her hobbies include cake decorating, ballet and traveling. She collects frogs, but does not kiss them. Carole says she's in love with life; she hopes the books she writes reflect this.

Prologue

With the storm, came the dream.

"Dawn." Her lover's voice was low and husky. He brushed his lips down the line of her nose. "Sweet Dawn."

His mouth sought and found hers in a slow, searching caress. Her lips grew pliant, then parted. She felt the teasing nip of his teeth followed by the tantalizing sweep of his tongue. The kiss deepened and grew more demanding.

"I need you," her lover whispered. The silken bristle of his mustache tickled her fair, flushed skin. "I need you so much."

He kissed a path along the side of her neck, pausing for an instant at the spot where her pulse beat like the wings of a captive butterfly. He pressed his mouth against the softly shadowed hollow at the base of her slender throat.

She stroked her hands over his naked back, fingers charting the supple line of his spine. Her palms recorded the ripple and release of well-toned muscles beneath perspiration-sheened skin. She said something on a gasping intake of breath.

His name. Had she spoken his name?

Her breasts were bare. Her lover covered them with his hands, massaging the sensitive flesh with unmistakable possessiveness. She quivered as hot, honeyed ribbons of sensation unfurled within her. She shook her head, the silken strands of her sun-gilded hair moving against her shoulders.

He traced the rose-pink aureoles of her nipples with his fingers, circling inward by tiny, tortuous increments. She bit her lip, shuddering, when he finally brushed the aching, eager peaks. She clung to him, her nails biting delicately into his broad shoulders. He made a sound—half groan, half growl—deep in his throat.

He licked the velvety crest of her right breast once... twice...three times. He nibbled at the throbbing bud of flesh with exquisite care, then licked it again. After a few moments, he transferred his attentions to her left breast, arousing and assuaging with tongue and teeth. She captured his head between her palms, her fingers tangling in his thick hair. She tried to say something. Whether it was a plea or a protest, she didn't know. The words were as broken as her breathing pattern and she was beyond piecing them back together.

"Yes. Oh, yes," her lover murmured, then sucked her left nipple into the hot, hungry depths of his mouth. The tugging pressure triggered a convulsive fluttering in her belly. She arched, her body going as taut as a bowstring. A wave of pleasure washed over her.

After many sweet and searing seconds, he returned to her right breast. She cried out as he claimed her with his lips once again. Desire danced through her bloodstream on fiery slippers.

Her lover caressed her with long, languid strokes. He discovered her with clever, questing fingers. He affirmed the willowy slenderness of her waist and admired the womanly swell of her hips. The hands that moved over her spoke eloquently of her beauty and made her believe in it.

"Oh." A gentle sigh.

"*Oh!*" A jolt of surprise.

"Dawn." Her lover's voice was rough, almost raw, with passion. "Lovely Dawn. No one...no one else..."

He was so strong. So very male. She skimmed her palms over the sweat-slick surface of his skin, once again testing the restless power and resilience of the muscles beneath. She felt him shudder, heard him catch his breath, and experienced a dizzying sense of feminine power. Angling her head, she pressed her lips against the hard line of his shoulder. She flicked her tongue lightly against the spot where she'd kissed and tasted the salt of his perspiration.

His hands slid to her inner thighs, thumbs finessing the smooth, honey gold flesh with sensual appreciation. She shifted her hips in an ancient and instinctive movement of invitation. He moved his hands upward slowly... very slowly.

"Yes," she whimpered, trembling with anticipation. "Please, yes."

She loved this man so much. She loved him, yet she had lied to him. No, not lied...exactly. But she *had* withheld her true self and offered a fantasy in its place.

She was not what he thought she was. Not really. Half of her desperately wished she could be. The other half—

"Mommy?"

A child's voice in the night. Soft. A little shaky. It was a sound she listened for even in the depths of slumber. It was a sound she heard with her heart.

Dreamy rapture gave way to stormy reality.

Elyssa Dawn Collins awoke, her eyes fluttering open. A flash of lightning illuminated her bedroom for a moment or two. She blinked against silvery brightness and the ghostly afterimages it sent shimmering across her field of vision.

"Mommy?"

Elyssa turned over. Standing by the edge of the bed, her small hands fisted in the tangle of pale blue sheets, was a long-haired little girl in a candy-striped nightgown. Her brown eyes were wide, her lower lip a bit wobbly.

"S-Sandy?" Elyssa questioned throatily, levering herself into a sitting position and brushing her fair hair out of her eyes. Her movements were as unsteady as her voice. She was aware of a tightness in her breasts and a sensation of emptiness lower down in her body. The ache—the feeling of frustration—were shamefully familiar.

The dream. She'd had the dream again.

Drawing a shaky breath, Elyssa pushed this humiliating realization out of her mind and concentrated on her daughter. "Did the storm wake you up, sweetie?" she asked.

The little girl nodded in a quick up-down movement that made her molasses brown hair ripple and bounce around her small shoulders. "I don't like it," she whispered.

"Oh, Sandy. Come here." Elyssa helped her daughter clamber up onto the bed, then hugged her tenderly. "Mommy doesn't like it much, either," she confided, kissing the top of the little girl's head.

There was another flash of lightning followed by a distant rumble of thunder. Elyssa felt Sandy tremble and tightened her embrace.

Sandy gave a soft sigh and cuddled closer. She smelled of soap and lemon shampoo. "Does it . . . does it make you scared, Mommy?" she asked in a hesitant voice after a few moments, plucking at the bedsheets.

Elyssa heard the unspoken plea for reassurance. At five-going-on-six, her daughter was desperate to put aside what she considered babyish behavior. If being afraid of a spring thunderstorm was something "big girls" weren't supposed to do, Sandy would pretend to be brave.

Elyssa would have fibbed in the cause of offering comfort, but there was no need to do that. Not this time. This time, she could answer her daughter's question with the truth.

"Yes, sweetie," she said softly, smoothing Sandy's tousled hair with gentle fingers. "It makes me scared."

Elyssa braced for the inevitable "Why?" but it didn't come. She breathed a silent prayer of thanks. Someday, she knew, she would have to tell her daughter everything. But not now, dear God. Please, not now.

The "everything" she had to tell was not for an innocent child's ears.

The "everything" was almost nothing at all.

If Sandy had asked why, Elyssa would have lied to her. She would have lied to her as she'd lied to nearly everyone else for more than six and a half years.

The few people to whom she'd tried to tell the truth hadn't believed her. Deep in her heart, she couldn't really blame them. She didn't want to believe the truth herself.

The truth was, Elyssa Dawn Collins was "scared" of storms because they made her dream. She dreamed the same dream each and every time. It was an erotic dream so intensely real it brought her to physical release.

The lover in her storm-inspired dream was a man who possessed her intimately. Utterly. Absolutely. Yet he was also a stranger whose name she didn't know and whose face she couldn't remember once she woke up.

The lover...the stranger...was the father of her only child.

One

———

Alexander Moran believed that bad news, like good Scotch, should be taken straight.

He heard papers being shuffled behind him and knew that his friend and personal lawyer, Philip Lassiter, had just placed another manila file folder on his desk.

How many similar folders had he seen during the past six years? he wondered with a flash of frustration. *How many?*

Alex didn't know. He'd lost count of the exact number long ago. But what did it matter? None of the scores of folders Philip had hand-delivered to him over the years had contained the information he was seeking.

"Tell me, Philip," he ordered evenly, staring out one of the floor-to-ceiling windows of his office. It was a glorious April morning on the other side of the glass. The sky above midtown Manhattan was a cloudless, celestial blue. It was free of any hint of the spring thunderstorm that had drenched the city and disturbed his sleep the night before. The color of the sky was so pure, so beautiful, it almost hurt to look at it.

Alexander Moran had once known a woman whose eyes were the same breathtaking hue. She was a woman he would give anything—anything—to see again.

The taupe-colored carpeting in his spacious, fifty-fifth floor office was thick, muffling the footsteps of anyone who walked across it. Alex sensed, rather than heard, his lawyer and friend approach him from behind. It occurred to him suddenly that Philip Lassiter was one of the few people in the world to whom he would willingly offer his unguarded back. He trusted Philip as he trusted no one else.

Philip cleared his throat. "The agency finally traced the helicopter pilot we believe evacuated...Dawn...off Isla de la Corazón after the hurricane," he said.

One corner of Alex's mind registered the fractional pauses that bracketed Philip's use of Dawn's name. The tiny hesitations had become familiar over the years and he'd occasionally speculated about the reason for them. He wondered if his friend had somehow picked up on the stab of emotion he experienced each time he heard the single syllable that encapsulated all he understood of ecstasy...and anguish. Alex knew it was irrational, but he hated the idea of Dawn's name falling from another man's lips. Any man's lips. Even Philip's.

"And?" he prompted, still gazing out at the magnificent view of Manhattan. From where he stood, he could see two buildings he owned and another half-dozen he'd helped build.

"The pilot's name was Sam Norcross," the lawyer went on. "He learned to fly helicopters in the military. He had some problems once he got out of the service. Couldn't keep a job. Moved around a lot. He ended up working for some...ahem...questionable people in the Caribbean. He wasn't flying under his own name at the time of the hurricane, which is one reason why he was so difficult to trace. The agency had to—"

"Skip the background," Alex interrupted. He knew what was coming. His friend had been speaking of Sam Norcross exclusively in the past tense. "Just give me the bottom line."

"He's dead, Alex."

Alex realized he'd clenched his hands into fists. He wanted to lash out. To smash something...or someone. He fought down the atavistic impulse toward violence, then forced himself to relax his fingers.

"How?" he asked, keeping his voice steady.

"A drunk-driving accident. There's a copy of the police report in the file if you want to read it."

Alex didn't want to open the file, much less read the police report it contained. "When?"

"Two weeks ago."

Alex remained silent. Two weeks, he reflected bitterly. Just fourteen days. Perhaps if he'd pushed harder or paid more, the investigators he'd hired would have located Sam Norcross sooner. And if they'd done that...

Stop it! he ordered himself. The man was dead and buried. Whatever he'd known about Dawn—if he'd known anything at all—had gone to the grave with him. No amount of second-guessing could change that.

"I'm sorry," Philip continued after a few moments. "Sam Norcross was the best lead we had. I wish there was something I could say or do—"

"There is," Alex cut in abruptly. He understood Philip's need to cushion hard truths with comforting words and acts of kindness. He truly did. But he wasn't ready to accept the other man's sympathy. He had enough difficulty accepting his help. "You can tell the agency to go back to square one and start over."

Alex couldn't fault his friend for believing in the power of good manners and good deeds any more than he could fault a five-year-old for believing in Santa Claus. Philip Lassiter—heir to a blue-blooded tradition and gilt-edged trust fund—was a soft man. Not a weak one. In fact, in terms of personal integrity, Philip was probably one of the strongest people Alex had ever known. But he was still soft. Untempered.

Alexander Moran was not a soft man and he knew it. At thirty-six, he was a few years younger than Philip Lassiter chronologically, but he was decades older in terms of what he had had to do in order to survive and succeed.

He'd struggled his way up from some of the meanest streets in the South Bronx. He'd never believed in Santa Claus or the Easter Bunny or the Tooth Fairy. He'd sweated away his boyhood for honest dimes while steeling himself against the lure of dishonest dollars, and he'd come of age with faith in nothing but his own ability to achieve against the odds.

That faith had not been misplaced.

Softness had always seemed the ultimate luxury to Alex. Even when he'd reached the point where he probably could have afforded it, he'd never really understood nor appreciated it. Softness was something he'd indulged in only once in his life. He was still paying the price for it.

Philip cleared his throat once again. "You want the agency to continue with the investigation?" he asked carefully.

"Yes," Alex affirmed without inflection.

"But—"

"They take my money, Philip. They take my orders."

"It—this isn't a question of money or orders."

"This isn't a question, period."

"Alex, please." Dismay frayed the normally patrician smoothness of Philip's voice. "After all this time, all this effort, there's nothing. Nothing! And I'm sorry for that. You know I'm sorry. But I think...dammit, I think you finally have to consider the possibility that she—that Dawn—"

Alex turned in one swift and savage movement. At six foot one, he topped his friend and lawyer by nearly five inches. He also outweighed him by forty pounds, all of it muscle.

The color drained from Philip's face and his expression altered radically, but he stood his ground.

"You think I finally have to consider the possibility that *what?*" Alex demanded, his voice as edged and sharp as a surgeon's scalpel. "That Dawn's dead? For God's sake, Philip! I've lived with that possibility for more than six and a half years. It gnaws at me every minute of every hour of every day. I also live with the possibility that Dawn's alive and well and doesn't want me to find her."

Philip made a conciliatory gesture. He was still very pale. "Alex, I know how you feel—"

"No, you don't," Alex disputed harshly, shaking his head. A lock of nut-brown hair curved down over his forehead. He brushed it back. "You can't even *imagine* how I feel. Until I met Dawn, I had no idea I could care for a woman the way I cared for her. She filled a void I didn't even know was there. The ten days we had together on Corazón were—were—" He broke off, searching for the right words to describe the indescribable.

"I was reborn because of Dawn," he finally went on. "I became a different person with her. And it didn't matter that she wouldn't tell me her full name or where she came from. God knows, I didn't tell her everything there was to know about me! Yes, she had secrets she wasn't ready to share. But I knew there'd come a time when she *would* be ready. A time when she'd trust me with the truth about herself. And I was willing to wait for that time, Philip. For the first time in my life, I was willing to wait for something to be given to me, rather than going out and taking it for myself."

Alex paused for a moment, studying his friend's face, wondering if he was making any sense. Articulating his feelings was something he found extraordinarily difficult to do. Contrary to what he knew most people believed about him, this was not because he didn't have any.

Alex had learned young that emotions made him weak when he needed to be strong and clouded his mind when he needed to be clearheaded. So, he'd set out to discipline— even deny—his intensely passionate nature. It had been a long and sometimes painful process. But, in the end, he had mastered himself.

His self-control had worked to his advantage over the years. It had given him an edge over people that he had never hesitated to use.

Never, that is, until he'd met a young woman who'd told him her name was Dawn. What he'd experienced in his heart and soul—in his gut and groin—in the first moments of that meeting had not been subject to discipline or denial.

Alex raked the fingers of one hand back through his razor-cut hair, still scrutinizing Philip's face. There was an expression in the other man's eyes he'd glimpsed a few times before. The first time he'd seen it had been when, after weeks of silent torment, he'd finally broken down, told Philip the story of what had happened on Isla de la Corazón, and asked for his help in trying to locate Dawn.

Alex pivoted back to the window again. He reached out and touched the cool, colorless glass.

She's out there somewhere, he told himself. *She has to be.*

Alex closed his eyes for a moment. He could visualize her so clearly. A fair-skinned, heart-shaped face framed by a tumble of champagne blond hair. Beautiful blue eyes. Ripe, rosy lips. An elegant nose with an incongruous dusting of freckles.

Alex opened his eyes.

"Do you think I'm crazy, Philip?" he asked abruptly.

Philip came to stand next to him. "You're the sanest man I know."

"Which doesn't rule out the possibility that you think I'm crazy."

"True," Philip conceded. He waited a beat or two, as though debating the wisdom of what he was about to say very carefully. Then he continued quietly, "But what I think doesn't make much of a difference in this case. Does it, Alex?"

Alex inhaled sharply. His friend had a way of knifing through to the heart of a matter when he least expected it.

"No," he answered after several seconds. "In this case, what you—or anybody else—thinks doesn't matter a damn."

There was a short silence.

"I'll tell the agency to keep looking," Philip promised.

A few moments later, Alex was alone.

Alone had seemed to him to be the natural order of things until a dazzling day in September more than six and a half years before. Oh, he'd come to that day having cultivated plenty of business associates and social acquaintances. And he'd discovered a friend he'd never expected to find in Philip Lassiter. He'd also coupled and uncoupled with enough women to have earned himself a reputation as a man who played almost as hard as he worked. Still, he'd basically defined his existence in solitary terms.

Then he'd met Dawn, and his definition of existence...and everything else...had been altered beyond recognition.

Slowly, Alex reached inside his charcoal gray suit jacket and extracted a black calfskin billfold. The billfold contained several hundred dollars in crisp currency, two credit cards, and a badly water-stained photograph of a blondhaired woman and a brown-haired man gazing into each other's eyes.

The woman was wearing a flamingo pink sarong that revealed her shoulders and the soft upper swell of her breasts. There was a spray of orchids in her cornsilk cloud of hair. She was smiling.

The man was wearing an open-collared white linen shirt and jeans. He was smiling, too, his teeth flashing white beneath his dark mustache.

Alex removed the wrinkled photograph from its thin plastic sheath very carefully, then cradled it in the palm of his right hand. He stared down at the tattered keepsake, remembering...

Dawn and he had been lingering over dinner at the small beachfront hotel where they'd each had a room. They'd known each other for five days. They had not yet become lovers, but they'd both known they would.

Their meal that evening had been spiced with anticipation. They'd eaten from each other's fingers, vying to share the tastiest tidbits and tenderest morsels of food. They'd played teasing games with feet and knees beneath the table. They'd laughed with the giddy innocence of children until the breathless moment when a flirtatious exchange of glances had suddenly flared into something very, very adult.

He'd felt his pulse throb, his blood thicken. He'd spoken her name in a husky voice.

She'd said his name in return. He'd watched the cool, crystalline blue of her wide-set eyes heat and turn hazy.

And then:

"I take a picture, *señor?*"

A skinny island boy—ten, maybe eleven—had materialized by their table. He'd had a Polaroid camera in his hands and a wary look in his dark eyes.

Alex had rounded on the youngster, angry at the intrusion. The anger had dissipated as he'd instinctively gauged the boy's hunger and hustle and felt an entirely unexpected flash of empathy.

"What?" he'd asked.

"A picture," the boy had repeated, relaxing just a little. "I take one for you. *Con su mujer.*" He'd darted a quick glance in Dawn's direction. "*Ella es muy hermosa, señor.*"

"Alex?" Dawn had questioned, sounding slightly bemused.

Alex had picked up a smattering of Spanish over the years. Although the bulk of his vocabulary was better suited for cursing than conversation, he'd known enough of the language to understand what the boy had said.

"He thinks you're mine and that you're very beautiful," he'd translated softly and watched Dawn blush.

The boy had nodded his agreement, then shrewdly pressed his sales pitch. "You want a picture, *sí?*"

Alex had already decided that *sí,* he wanted a picture very much. But he'd realized he was expected to bargain before buying.

"How much?"

"*Solamente cinco dólares americanos.*"

"Five dollars?" Alex had smiled fleetingly at the youngster's highball approach to pricing. "*Uno.*"

"*Oh, señor, no. No. Cuatro.*"

"*Dos.*"

"*Tres. Es muy barato.* Very cheap."

"Done."

So, the price had been paid and the picture taken. Alex and Dawn had watched their images condense out of nothingness on the glossy white square that had been produced by the camera.

They'd been looking at each other when the boy had snapped the shutter. They'd looked at each other again when the photograph had finished developing.

Again, he'd spoken her name.

Again, she's said his in return.

"Yes?" he'd asked, reaching across the table to take her hand.

"Yes," she'd answered, her fingers interlacing with his.

Dawn had given herself to him for the first time that night. She'd given herself freely. Absolutely. And he had given himself to her in exactly the same way.

Less than a week later, they'd survived a storm that had left Isla de la Corazón—the Island of the Heart—broken. They'd survived it together only to be separated once the skies had cleared.

"I'll be back," he'd promised the last time he'd seen her. He hadn't wanted to leave, but he'd had knowledge that had been desperately needed elsewhere. Knowledge that had literally made the difference between life and death for nearly a dozen people.

"I'll be waiting," she'd replied.

But she hadn't been.

When he'd returned forty-eight exhausting hours later, Dawn had been gone. He'd managed to piece together an incomplete and often contradictory story involving falling debris, some kind of injury, and a helicopter evacuation to an unknown location.

He'd discovered the photograph of the two of them in the windblown wreckage of the bungalow they'd shared for five passionate nights. It had been the only tangible proof of Dawn's existence he'd ever found.

Alex slipped the snapshot back into his billfold.

He'd been searching for Dawn for more than six and a half years.

He still didn't know who she was.

Or what had happened to her.

But he was going to find out.

For better or for worse, no matter how much time or money it took, he was going to find out.

The ladies' room at Carradine and Associates was empty for once and for this Elyssa Collins was profoundly grateful. She needed to be alone for a few minutes.

She massaged her temples with her fingertips. She'd woken that morning with what she could only describe as a hangover from the erotic intoxication of her storm-inspired dream. She'd experienced such hangovers before. They usually faded away after a few hours. But this one hadn't eased in the slightest as the day had worn on. If anything, it had intensified.

You've got to pull yourself together! she instructed herself firmly. *You've got to be on your toes for this afternoon's meeting.*

Elyssa studied her image critically in the wall-length mirror mounted above the powder room's row of sinks. She looked marginally better than she felt, she decided. Of course, the lighting she was examining herself under was extraordinarily flattering. After all, Carradine and Associates was one of New York City's most innovative interior design firms. The company was not about to subject its female employees to the soul-depressing effects of ordinary fluorescent illumination.

Opening her purse, Elyssa took out a monogrammed silver compact and began touching up her makeup. Covering the freckles on her nose was easy. Masking the smudgy shadows beneath her eyes required considerably more work. After a minute or so of dabbing and patting, she put the compact away and turned her attention to her hair.

She'd worn her pale blond hair long for most of her life, letting it tumble loose to the middle of her back. She'd cut it short roughly six and a half years before, just days after her arrival in New York City. A new life, a new hairstyle, she'd told herself as she'd wielded the scissors.

Looking back, Elyssa strongly suspected that chopping off her hair had been a substitute for having some kind of breakdown.

She frowned suddenly, not wanting to remember how frightened and fragile she'd felt during her first months on her own in New York. And then, just when she'd started to find her feet, she'd been knocked off balance by the awful ordeal of Sandy's premature birth. She didn't want to remember that, either.

Elyssa fluffed her hair, which was currently styled to fall a bit above her shoulders, with fingers that weren't quite steady. There were a great many things in her twenty-seven years of life she didn't want to remember.

The death of her father.

The displeasure of the man her mother had married afterward.

The betrayal of her fiancé.

What she'd done and whom she'd done it with on a Caribbean island called—

Elyssa slammed the brake on this train of thought, utterly appalled at the direction it had taken.

What she'd done and whom she'd done it with.

Elyssa clenched her hands and closed her eyes, struggling for control.

She wanted to remember, she told herself fiercely. She did! Dear Lord, she had a two-week hole in the fabric of her life. How could she *not* want to repair it? How could she not want to know exactly what had happened during the fourteen days between the morning she'd gotten on a plane in Chicago and the evening she'd woken up in a hospital in Galveston?

And yet . . .

And yet, deep down, she knew she was afraid of filling in the blanks. She was afraid of having her darkest suspicions about her behavior confirmed. She was ashamed, too. Ashamed of the possibilities, the probabilities, evoked by the dream she'd had the night before.

Bang!

Elyssa started violently as the door to the ladies' room burst open and a petite brunette in her mid-thirties stomped in.

"I can't stand it anymore!" the intruder announced shrilly, waving bangle-laden arms. The door crashed shut behind her. "I simply cannot stand it anymore! I *told* her the leather was a mistake. I begged her to use lacquer. I ruined a twelve dollar pair of designer panty hose going down on my knees to plead with her. Did she listen? No-o-o-o-o-o. Of course not. *She* thought leather would make a statement about her personality. Statement, hah! Personality, double hah! The place looks like the headquarters for some S-and-M—" The woman broke off in mid-rave, apparently registering Elyssa's presence for the first time. Her manner went from bellicose to benign in a twinkling.

"Oh, hi, Lys," she said in a pleasant voice. She waggled fingers tipped with beautifully manicured, blood red nails.

"Hi, Nikki," Elyssa responded with a mixture of amusement and affection. The woman she was addressing was Nikki Spears. Nikki was one of the chief designers at Carradine and Associates. She was outrageously talented and outrageously temperamental. She was also a woman whose friendship Elyssa had come to cherish over the past six years.

Nikki crossed to the row of sinks, the three-inch heels of her alligator pumps clicking against the marble floor tiles. "I'm having a few problems with a client," she commented as she shrugged off the leather tote she had slung over her left shoulder.

"I never would have guessed," Elyssa responded with a fleeting smile. She'd once overheard a co-worker claim that having an encounter with Nikki Spears was like having electroshock treatment. She had to concede that there was a certain validity to the description.

Nikki reached into her voluminous shoulder bag. Like most of the rest of her ensemble, it was fashionably, funereally, black. She pulled out a can of nonaerosol hair spray and began spritzing her dark, artfully cropped tresses.

"So, how are you doing today, Lys?" she queried after several moments.

"I'm fine," Elyssa responded automatically.

The brunette gave her a sharp look. "Really? You look a little stressed out."

Elyssa felt a flutter of anxiety. She'd suspected for a long time that Nikki probably doubted—possibly just plain didn't believe—the story she'd spun about herself when she'd arrived in New York. While her friend had never di rectly challenged her claim of having been married young, then been left widowed with a baby on the way, she'd asked more than a few difficult-to-answer questions over the years.

There had been moments when the urge to respond to those questions by confiding the truth had been very strong, but Elyssa had always resisted it. While she was certain her friend would take the revelation that Sandy had been born out of wedlock in stride, she was less sanguine about Nikki's reactions to some of the other secrets she was keeping.

"I'm fine," Elyssa repeated, sustaining the other woman's gaze steadily. "And if I look stressed out, it's because of the Moranco presentation."

Nikki's brown eyes widened. "Oh, God!" she gasped. "That's this afternoon, isn't it! I've been so crazed about my own projects, I completely forgot. No wonder you're a little frayed around the edges. I mean, it's *only* the company's biggest commercial commission of the year. Is everything all squared away for the meeting?"

Elyssa pushed back the sleeve of the loose-fitting navy jacket she was wearing and glanced at her watch. "I'm supposed to go over and help with the setup in about thirty minutes," she replied. Although the Moranco presentation was not the most soothing of subjects, she was relieved by the shift from the personal to the professional.

Nikki stuffed the can of hair spray into her bag and started rooting around for something else. "So, while I'm consulting with the Wicked Witch of the West Side about toning down her whips and chains decor, you'll be having a tête-à-tête with one of the Big Apple's most eligible bachelors, hmm?"

"I don't think so, Nikki."

"What?" Nikki produced a small bottle of cologne from the depths of her leather tote. She gave Elyssa a teasing look. "You don't think the tall, dark, handsome, and rich Alexander Moran is one of the most eligible bachelors in the city?"

"I don't think I'm going to be having a tête-à-tête with him," Elyssa responded dryly. An odd frisson had skittered up her spine at the mention of Alexander Moran's name. She put it down to nerves. "I'm going to be the least senior member of the design team at the meeting, remember?"

"Which means our fearless leader will expect you to pass sketches and keep your mouth shut," Nikki translated ruefully. "I know the drill, believe me. Humpty Dumpty is *such* a sexist."

"Nikki!" Elyssa couldn't really disagree with the characterization of their employer, Homer Carradine. But she did wish her friend would refrain from calling the man Humpty Dumpty. Sandy had coined the nickname in all innocence after visiting her mother's place of work one afternoon. Nikki had decided it was hilariously on-target and appropriated it.

"Well, he is," Nikki insisted, blithely ignoring Elyssa's admonition. She opened the cologne bottle and spent a good thirty seconds applying the fragrance to various pulse points. Then her mouth quirked wickedly and she inquired, "Wouldn't you like to, though?"

Elyssa had no idea how to respond to this apparent non sequitur. She'd become extremely familiar with her friend's zigzagging approach to conversation over the years. Unfortunately becoming familiar with it and being able to follow it were two different things.

"Wouldn't I like to what?" she asked cautiously.

Nikki put the top back on the cologne bottle. "Have a tête-à-tête with Alexander Moran, of course. Wouldn't you like to? *I* certainly would!"

"Well, I..." Elyssa hesitated, oddly disconcerted by what Nikki was suggesting. "I've never really considered it," she answered after a moment, then found herself wondering if she'd told the truth. While she'd never met Carradine and Associates' most important new client, there was no denying that he'd been in her thoughts on more than a few occasions.

She'd first become aware of Alexander Moran's existence not too long after Sandy had been born. She'd been leafing through a magazine and suddenly found herself riveted by the photograph of a dark-haired man with angular features and an intense, almost angry, expression.

The man had been Alexander Moran, and he'd been the subject of a two-page piece titled "An Up-and-Comer Turns Comet."

There had been a great many other articles in the ensuing years. While Elyssa certainly hadn't made any conscious effort to keep track of them, she'd read quite few. She'd learned that Alexander Moran had dug foundations in his teens, formed a construction company in his twenties, and started buying buildings before he turned thirty. Press reports described him as street smart, driven, and almost impossible to get to know.

"Lys?"

Elyssa blinked and shook her head. "What?"

"Are you considering it now?"

"I—what?"

Nikki rolled her eyes in exasperation. "Are you considering having a tête-à-tête with Alexander Moran?"

Elyssa heard the ladies' room door open and decided it was time to close the subject under discussion.

"For heaven's sake, Nikki," she said. "I haven't even been introduced to the man!"

Alex strode down the corridor toward the Moranco conference room with a feeling of anticipation. The project at hand represented a new challenge for him and he relished that. Even though he was obsessed by a piece of his past, he needed to keep moving forward.

He'd acquired a medium-sized Manhattan hotel two months before in a deal that still gave him a sense of satisfaction to contemplate. The once ultrastylish establishment had slid into a state of extreme shabbiness over the years, then been driven to the brink of bankruptcy by a fire. The owners had been discussing closing the place down when he'd approached them with an offer they couldn't refuse.

His intention was to restore the hotel to its former glory and reopen it. That's why he'd hired Carradine and Associates.

Alex reached his destination. He opened one of the double doors to the conference room and walked in.

His entrance went unnoticed for a few moments, which suited him perfectly. He scanned the dozen or so people

present, noting that the members of his staff were outnum-
bered by the employees of Carradine and Associates.

And then, without the slightest hint of warning, he spotted her. She was standing at the far end of the room, fid-
dling with a slide projector.

Every masculine instinct he had exploded to life.

Her hair was shorter than it had been and it had swung
forward to veil her face, but Alex knew her.

She was dressed as he'd never seen her dressed. The sensual slenderness of the body that had fit his so perfectly was
hidden by the loose cut of her clothes, but still Alex knew
her.

Dawn.

Alex started to walk forward. He had to concentrate on
each and every step. His entire body seemed to have gone
into shock. His heart was slamming against the inside of his
chest like a sledgehammer. The air he was trying to breathe
burned his nostrils and lungs.

He felt a hand clasp his arm. Heard a voice say his name.

"Mr. Moran! So good to see you again."

He looked blankly at the balding, rather rotund man
who'd just spoken to him. "Mr. Carradine," he responded
automatically, having absolutely no idea which part of his
brain had supplied the identification.

"Let me introduce my team."

"I—"

Carradine insisted. Alex acquiesced, keeping his attention fixed on the only person in the room who mattered.

"This is David Schiff...Jessica Orth...Wexler Daley..."

"Hello...how are you...hello..."

Dawn didn't seem to register his presence until he came
within touching distance. In the instant before she lifted her
head and he could finally see her face, he caught the faint
smell of her perfume. The delicately floral fragrance was
unfamiliar to him. Dawn had never worn perfume on Isla
de la Corazón.

"And this is Elyssa Collins," Homer Carradine announced. "Elyssa, Alexander Moran."

Alex had thought he'd imagined every possible variation of this moment. He learned in the space of a single heartbeat that he hadn't.

"Elyssa...Collins?" he asked. The name caught in his throat and felt strange on his tongue.

"That's right," Elyssa answered in the contralto voice that had haunted him for more than six and a half years. Her gentle, generous lips curved in a tentative smile. She held out her hand. "How do you do, Mr. Moran."

Her eyes—Dawn's eyes—were still blue. Still beautiful.

The last time Alexander Moran had gazed into those beautiful blue eyes, they'd been filled with love and longing and more than a little fear for his safety.

Now, they seemed full of questions.

They did not contain a flicker of recognition.

Two

_____

"**A**re you all right, Mr. Moran?"

The inquiry could have been asked in some obscure African dialect for all the sense it made to Alex. He checked himself in midstride and looked at Dorothy Reynolds, his secretary of ten years. He saw her plump shoulders stiffen beneath the jacket of her beige linen suit.

"What?" he asked harshly.

"Are you all right?" she repeated.

Alex almost laughed. He was a lot of things at this moment, but all right wasn't one of them.

"I'll live," he answered tersely.

"You, ah, you asked me earlier to remind you that you have an appointment with—"

"Cancel it."

"But, Mr. Howlett's office called just five minutes ago. He's already on his—"

"Cancel the appointment, Mrs. Reynolds," Alex ordered in a voice that was as flat and cold as a slab of marble in winter. "And hold my calls until further notice."

Dorothy Reynolds' throat worked convulsively for a few moments as she knit and unknit her fingers. "Yes, sir," she said finally.

Alex acknowledged her reply with a curt nod, then proceeded into his office.

Once inside, he crossed to the small wet bar built into one corner of the sun-filled room and poured a slug of Scotch into a heavy leaded crystal glass. He knocked the liquor back in a single gulp, letting it burn a smoky path down his throat and into his belly.

He repeated the procedure again, and again after that. His movements were rhythmic and precise. He didn't waste a motion. He didn't spill a drop.

The fourth time Alex poured, he didn't drink. He stopped, the glass barely an inch from his lips. The peaty odor of the liquor assailed his nostrils.

He gripped the edge of the built-in bar with his free hand. While he was a long, long way from being falling down drunk, he suddenly felt very weak in the knees. His head pounded sickeningly. His vision blurred for an instant, then cleared. Summoning up lessons learned over the years, he struggled to control the emotions roiling through him.

Count. One. Two. Three. Four.

The glass in his fist was the finest crystal, the Scotch it contained was an imported single malt. Alex found himself recalling the days when it had stretched his budget almost to the breaking point to buy a six-pack of beer.

Count. Five. Six. Seven. Eight.

Abruptly, Alex let go of the bar. Pivoting smoothly on one foot, he hurled the glass of Scotch across the room. The raging curse that erupted from the bottom of his soul blended with the sound of shattering crystal.

Count. Nine. Ten.

Alex stood for a few moments, staring at the liquor-stained wall opposite him. He shuddered like a man in the grip of a tropical fever, then shifted his gaze downward. Jagged shards of glass winked mockingly in the lush nap of the brownish gray carpet.

"Oh . . . God," he groaned. "Oh, Dawn."

She didn't remember him! The woman he'd been seeking for more than six and a half years didn't remember him! She'd smiled, said his name, and extended her hand to him as though he were a total stranger!

But how could that be? *How?*

All right. Yes. His appearance had changed with the passage of time. He'd shaved his mustache and gone a bit gray at the temples. He also knew his face and body had acquired some signs of wear and tear over the years. But he hadn't changed that much! Dawn's appearance had altered more than his had. Yet he had known who she was the split second he'd laid eyes on her.

Had the time they'd had together on Isla de la Corazón meant so little to her? he asked himself. Had the days and nights that had altered the course of his existence been of such minor significance to her that she could put them—and the man she'd shared them with—completely out of her mind?

Alex felt as though he were choking. An ugly, acrid taste filled his mouth. He jerked loose the knot of his tie, then yanked open the top three buttons of his shirt.

"Damn her!" he swore, spitting out the words as though trying to purge himself of some poison. He balled his right hand into a fist and slammed it down. "Damn her to hell!"

The words seemed to hang in the air. Accusing him. Accusing her. Alex heard them echoing inside his skull. After a few moments, the anger drained out of him. He slumped a little, bowing his head and closing his eyes.

No, he thought painfully. He couldn't damn her. Oh, he could say the words. He could scream them aloud until his throat bled if he wanted to. But he couldn't—wouldn't—mean them. He couldn't damn Dawn and he couldn't damn Elyssa Collins, either.

Slowly, Alex opened his eyes.

"Elyssa Collins," he said aloud, testing the sound of each syllable, discovering an unexpected hint of music in every one. Then, yearningly, he whispered, "Dawn."

Could she have been *pretending* not to know him? Alex turned this idea over in his mind. It was a possibility he had to consider because, for all her apparent lack of recognition, Elyssa Collins had had a very strong reaction to him.

He'd felt her hand tremble when he'd taken it in his. He'd seen a hot flush of color stain her cheeks at the same moment. He'd heard her catch her breath as well.

And her response hadn't ended there. She'd been intensely aware of him during the meeting. He'd known it by the way she'd kept shifting in her seat, patting at her hair, and nibbling on her lower lip. What's more, each time he'd been forced to turn his eyes away from her, he'd sensed the touch of her gaze on him. He'd never caught her looking, but there was no question in his mind that she had been.

But *why* would she pretend? he wondered, forking his fingers through his hair. What possible motive could she have for doing so?

Alex frowned, shaking his head and thinking of the photograph resting within the billfold inside his jacket. After more than six and a half years of searching, he'd finally found her. He'd finally found . . . Dawn.

He *still* didn't know who she was. Not really.

But he was going to find out.

Alex moved to his desk with long, swift strides. He hit the switch on the intercom that connected him to his secretary.

"Dorothy?" He thought he heard a quick intake of breath on the other end.

"Ah, yes, Mr. Moran?"

"Get Carradine and Associates on the line for me."

"Carradine and Associates. Yes, sir. Right away."

Alex was about to turn the intercom off when he recalled his earlier behavior. He grimaced, then said, "One other thing, Dorothy."

"Yes, sir."

"I apologize for the way I acted when I came in."

"Mr. Moran, you don't have to—"

"Yes, Dorothy, I do," he interrupted. "Now, please. Get me Carradine and Associates."

Elyssa had begun her career at Carradine and Associates sitting behind a reception desk. She'd eventually progressed to the firm's open "bullpen," an area where paper airplanes and take-out eggrolls were tossed around almost as frequently as design ideas. Roughly eighteen months before, she'd graduated to her own cubicle.

The partitioned-off work space didn't provide much in the way of amenities or elbow room, but it did offer a modicum of privacy. And privacy was what Elyssa very desperately needed right now. She hoped that spending a few minutes by herself would enable her to regain her equilibrium to the point where she could join the post-presentation celebration going on in Homer Carradine's office.

Nothing in her life—not even her storm-summoned dreams—had prepared her for the surge of attraction she'd felt when she'd turned and looked up into Alexander Moran's gold-flecked brown eyes. She'd experienced an instant, electric sense of connection that had made her body quiver and her breath wedge like a cork at the top of her throat.

Angles. Hard, hammered angles. They'd seemed to dominate the unyielding contours of Alexander Moran's lean, tanned face in the first instant she'd stared up into it. She'd had an impression of sharp cheekbones, a squared chin, and a nose that canted slightly left, as though it had once been broken.

His brown hair had been brushed back from his brow and touched with silver at both temples. His skin had been taut, but a little weathered by years of outdoor labor. There'd been a faint shadowing of new beard growth on his jaw, which had added to his potent aura of masculine toughness.

Elyssa swallowed hard, remembering the way he'd stared at her in the moments immediately after Homer Carradine had introduced them. The probing—almost predatory—intensity of Alexander Moran's gaze had shaken her to the core.

She'd extended her hand to him automatically, offering it along with a smile she'd felt fading away even as it formed. After what had seemed like an eternity of waiting, he'd grasped her hand with his own.

Elyssa shifted in her chair, trying to ignore the tiny, white-hot shivers running up and down her spine. Sweet heaven, the man had only touched her for a moment! she thought wildly. Yet the brief brush of his long fingers and the fleeting press of his hard palm had burned through her like a brand, sending a wave of hot blood flooding up into her cheeks.

The phone on her desk trilled suddenly. Elyssa gasped and went rigid. The phone trilled a second time and then a third. She finally picked up the receiver with a shaky hand and put it to her ear.

"Hello?" she asked throatily.

"Ms. Collins?"

There was no mistaking the identity of her caller. The deep, resonant voice was as compelling as the man to whom it belonged.

Elyssa gripped the phone very tightly. "Mr. Moran."

"You were expecting a call from me?" It was an odd question with an even odder edge to it.

"No. No, of course not," she denied.

"Then how—"

"I recognized your voice."

"Ah."

There was a pause.

"Mr. Moran?" Elyssa finally prompted. Why is he calling me? she wondered uneasily, twisting a lock of hair around one finger.

"I'd like you to have dinner with me, Ms. Collins."

"Dinner?"

"Yes. Tonight."

"If this is about the hotel project—"

"This is a personal invitation. Not a professional one."

There was something dark—almost dangerous—about the way he pronounced the word "personal."

"Oh," was all she could think of to say.

"Do you have another commitment?"

"What?" There was a small, silver-framed photograph of Sandy sitting on the corner of Elyssa's desk. Her eyes slewed toward the portrait, and she experienced an inexplicable flash of anxiety.

"Are you seeing someone else tonight?"

Anxiety gave way to indignation. She looked away from her daughter's picture.

"Mr. Moran—" she began, fully intending to inform the very disturbing man on the other end of the line that he had no right to ask her such a question in such a tone of voice. She broke off abruptly when she realized she was no longer alone. Nikki Spears was standing in the doorway of her work cubicle, hands on hips, head cocked, unabashedly eavesdropping.

"Moran?" the brunette hissed. "Alexander Moran?"

"Excuse me for a minute," Elyssa said hurriedly into the mouthpiece of the telephone, then covered it with her palm.

"Is that Alexander Moran?" her friend demanded.

"Nikki—"

"Is it?"

"Yes, but—"

"What does he want?"

"I—"

"A date? Does he want a date?" The volume of Nikki's voice increased by several significant decibels.

"Shhh!" Elyssa pleaded. "Yes. No. I don't know!" Somehow, the word "date" seemed far too adolescent to be applied to this situation. Whatever this situation was. "He wants me to have dinner with him."

"And?" The black-clad brunette was back to hissing again.

"And, I don't know him!"

"Well, he doesn't know you, either." The retort was instant and decidedly exasperated. "That's *probably* why he's asking you to have dinner with him. So you can get to know each other."

"But—"

"For heaven's sake, Lys!" Nikki waved her arms expansively, the bangles on her wrists clacking noisily. "You haven't been out with a man since you went to the ballet with my cousin, the podiatrist, a year ago. Now, I can see how Henry would put you off the opposite sex, but this is different."

Elyssa shook her head, her fair hair belling out slightly with the movement. "I can't do it."

"Why not?"

"He wants to have dinner with me *tonight*."

Her friend's brows arched. "What's wrong with tonight? I know for a fact you're not doing anything."

Elyssa glanced at her daughter's picture.

"I'll baby-sit Sandy," Nikki volunteered instantly. "Now, say yes!"

"I don't—"

"Ms. Collins?"

Elyssa caught her breath. The sound of Alexander Moran's distinctive voice sent a tremor through her nervous system. She realized with a shock that she wanted to succumb to his invitation and Nikki's insistence. She wanted to say . . . yes.

"Hello?"

She uncovered the mouthpiece of the phone, acutely aware that Nikki was nodding vehemently.

"I'm here." The steadiness of her reply surprised her.

"Problem?"

"No." She felt one corner of her mouth curl up. "A friend."

"I see."

Nikki was now mouthing the word "yes" over and over again.

"Mr. Moran—"

"Have dinner with me tonight," he interrupted. "Please . . . Elyssa."

Elyssa took a deep breath, then let it out very slowly. She turned her back on Nikki.

"All right," she agreed softly. "I will."

They met at a small French restaurant on the East Side about four hours later.

"I'm still not certain I should be doing this," Elyssa confessed with a little laugh. She picked up the long-stemmed glass to her right and took a quick sip of wine from it.

"Doing what?" Alex asked, tracking her movements like a hawk. He watched the downward flick of her long lashes as she drank and the subtle working of her throat as she swallowed. The wine left a faint but provocative sheen on her lips. He felt the lower part of his body start to tighten as he contemplated licking that sheen off with his tongue. "Having dinner?"

"Having dinner with a *client*."

He took a drink from his own glass. "Well, there's a simple remedy for that."

"There is?"

"Mmm," he affirmed with a casual nod. "I'll break my contract with Carradine and Associates. Stop being a client."

"Alex—" She spoke on a sharp intake of breath.

He felt a fierce jolt of satisfaction at her use of his given name. His reaction to the undisguised anxiety that stiffened her voice and shadowed her delicate features was entirely different.

"I was only joking, Elyssa."

Elyssa studied Alex without speaking for several seconds, her pulse beating out a peculiar hip-hop rhythm. She didn't know what to make of the expression in his compelling, whiskey-colored eyes. She glanced away.

"Only joking," she echoed. "I see."

Alex fought down a spurt of anger. Whether the emotion was directed at himself or at her or at the both of them together, he couldn't say.

"Do you honestly believe I'd do something like that?" he asked bluntly, struggling against the urge to reach across the table and force her face back toward his. Dammit, Dawn, he thought. You know I wouldn't. You *know* me!

Or did she? Alex was still a long way from figuring out whether the lovely woman sitting opposite him genuinely didn't remember him or whether she was only pretending she didn't. He was even further from deciding which scenario was worse.

Elyssa looked back at Alex, startled by the urgency of his question. His features were taut, and his broad shoulders looked braced to receive a blow.

"No," she denied after a moment, wondering why her opinion should matter so much to him. "No, of course not. It's just that—" she paused.

He pounced, a small muscle in his jaw jumping as he clenched his teeth. "Just that what?"

He was pushing her for some reason, and Elyssa didn't like the feeling. She'd let herself be emotionally bullied into a great many things when she'd been growing up. Not so much out of weakness or passivity, but because she'd desperately wanted to please people. It had taken her a long time, but she'd eventually come to understand how she'd allowed herself to be victimized by her need for approval. With that understanding—and the adversity that had brought it—had come the will to change.

While Elyssa seriously doubted she'd ever acquire the jump-in-with-both-feet assertiveness of someone like her friend, Nikki, she'd learned to stand up for herself during the past six and a half years. She'd discovered an inner strength she hadn't realized she'd had and she'd nurtured it along with her precious daughter. People who pushed her nowadays might not get pushed back, but they seldom made much progress shoving her in the direction of their choosing, either.

"Elyssa?" Alex prodded.

Lifting her chin a notch or two, Elyssa met his searching gaze squarely. She saw his gold-flecked eyes narrow, as though something about her manner had taken him by surprise.

"You have a reputation for getting what you want," she told him evenly. "In fact, I've heard—"

The arrival of their waiter forestalled the rest of her comment. Elyssa subsided into silence as the man bustled about, placing a portion of asparagus vinaigrette in front of her and a plate of iced oysters on the half-shell in front of Alex. After pouring a bit more wine into each of their glasses and ascertaining that no further service was immediately required, the waiter moved on to another table.

Elyssa picked up the smaller of the two forks to the left of her plate and prepared to taste her appetizer.

"'In fact'—what?'' Alex asked. Elyssa's flash of feistiness had caught him off balance. The woman he'd known on Isla de la Corazón had never shown that kind of spark. He'd sensed the potential for it. Indeed, that had been one of the many things that had attracted him to her. But she'd never met him head-on about anything during their ten days together.

"Nothing."

"Oh, no." Alex picked up one of the lemon wedges that had come with his plate and squeezed it over several of the oysters. "Don't back off now. Tell me what you've heard."

His tone was part challenge, part command. Elyssa bridled at both. Forking up a stalk of asparagus, she bit off the tip. She chewed it, barely registering the crisp texture of the lightly cook vegetable or the savory tang of the delicate dressing, then swallowed.

After a moment, she replied bluntly, "People say you can be ruthless."

If she'd been hoping to disconcert him, and she was not at all certain she had, she failed.

"True enough," Alex acknowledged. "Does that trouble you?"

"That you can be ruthless?"

"Mmm-hmm." He ate an oyster.

Elyssa finished the stalk of asparagus she'd forked up. She was conscious that her heart was beating faster than usual. She was not accustomed to dueling with a man while dining with him.

"I suppose that depends."

"On?"

"The situation."

"You believe in mitigating circumstances, then."

Elyssa hesitated, thinking about the lies she'd told and the deceptions she'd practiced during the past six and a half years. "I believe a person can be driven to ruthlessness . . . and other things," she told him honestly.

"Have you ever been?" he pressed.

"Hasn't everyone?" she parried, retreating from her comparative candor of just a moment before.

Alex's mouth thinned. *This* was the Dawn he'd known. Intelligent. Intriguing. And as elusive as quicksilver when it came to providing hard facts about herself.

On Isla de la Corazón, he'd wanted her to yield her secrets to him as willingly as she'd yielded her body. So, he'd trodden very, very gently with her. Now, however, his most primitive instincts were clamoring for him to put his foot down and put it down hard.

But what . . . what if this woman *weren't* Dawn? he asked himself suddenly. They said everyone had a twin somewhere in the world. Was it possible that there were two blue-eyed blondes who could create in him the kind of soul-stealing ache he was experiencing right now? Could he possibly be mistaken about who Elyssa Collins was?

Do you think I'm crazy, Philip? he'd asked his best friend that morning.

Do *I* think I'm crazy? he asked himself now.

God. Was it possible he'd wanted to find Dawn so desperately for so long that he'd finally snapped? Could he be imposing his dream on a stranger with a seemingly familiar face?

No. Alex rejected the idea. Dammit, no! Elyssa Collins *was* Dawn. He was certain of it.

"You seem to know much more about me than I know about you," he observed tightly. He swallowed another oyster, chasing it down with a quick gulp of wine.

Not for the first time, Elyssa had the distinct and disturbing impression that at least some of Alex's comments were like icebergs. What lurked below the surface of his words was far more significant than what he actually said aloud.

"Well, you *are* a public figure," she pointed out.

"You've followed my 'ruthless' career?"

"I've read some articles about you."

"The ones about how I went from digging ditches to buying buildings, no doubt."

Elyssa set down her fork and leaned forward, a frown wrinkling her brow. She didn't believe for a moment that Alex could be as indifferent to his accomplishments as his tone seemed to suggest. Yet there was obviously something gnawing at him, making him question their value.

"Aren't you proud of what you've done?" she questioned softly.

Alex's mouth twisted. "Sometimes I wonder why I did it."

She shook her head. "I find that very hard to believe."

"Why?"

"Because..." Elyssa paused, trying to shape a coherent answer out of confused emotions. How could she explain to the man sitting opposite her that, although she'd been introduced to him only hours before, she felt she knew and understood him? How could she explain it to him when she couldn't explain it to herself?

"Why, Elyssa?"

"Because you don't strike me as a man who does anything without a reason," she told him simply.

"You aren't married," he said without preamble a few minutes later. Their waiter had just departed after serving their entrées. He'd gone away in something of a snit, apparently insulted by the fact that both of them had left most of their appetizers uneaten.

Elyssa paused in the act of bringing a morsel of sole meunière to her lips. Intellectually, she knew he wasn't accusing her of anything. At a more visceral level, his words stung.

"I wouldn't be here if I were," she returned succinctly. "And I wouldn't be here if *you* were, either."

Alex remained silent for several seconds, registering the flicker of anger that had passed through Elyssa's blue eyes in reaction to his words. Infidelity—even the idea of it—obviously troubled his dinner companion.

"Have you ever been?"

"Yes." She reminded herself, as she'd done countless times before, that the lie was necessary. The reminder did nothing to improve the nasty taste the falsehood left in her mouth. She took a quick sip of wine.

"Divorced?"

"I'm a widow."

Elyssa could tell her words had shocked Alex. She hoped they'd shocked him enough to prevent him from probing further. She realized she didn't want to lie to this man any more than she had to. Bracing herself, she drank a bit more wine and waited.

Alex wasn't certain what to say. The information Elyssa had just disclosed was completely unexpected. He knew it was going to take him some time to adjust to it. He picked up his knife and fork slowly, then cut and ate a bite of the steak *au poivre* he'd ordered. The meat was juicily tender and skillfully spiced. He probably wouldn't have noticed if it had been salt-encrusted cowhide.

"Was he—your husband—from New York?" Half of him wanted to know everything there was to know about the man. The other half wanted to deny his existence.

Elyssa shifted in her seat and shook her head. "No. Chicago."

"Chicago?"

"I was born and raised near there." This, at least, had the benefit of being the truth.

He nodded, filing the tidbit of background away for future reference. "Is your family—?"

"My father died when I was eight. My mother still lives in the area."

"But you're not close to her." It wasn't a question. There'd been grief when she'd spoken of her father. A different kind of hurt when she'd mentioned her mother.

"No." Startled by Alex's perceptivity, Elyssa let the admission slip out. She then felt compelled to elaborate on it. "She remarried when I was ten. The man was—is—well, let's just say that nothing I've ever done has won his full approval."

No, that wasn't quite true, she amended silently. Paul Haywood *had* wholeheartedly endorsed her engagement to Lane Edwards more than seven years before. But what a disaster that had turned out to be!

Elyssa shook her head a little, trying to clear out the bad memories. She sampled another bite of the fish, then decided to steer the conversation in another direction. "What about your family?"

Alex surprised himself by accepting her very obvious bid to shift the focus of their discussion. He didn't make a practice of allowing himself to be sidetracked. "I don't have any," he answered.

"None at all?"

He shook his head. "No brothers. No sisters. No uncles. No aunts. My father walked out when I was three. My mother died when I was seventeen."

"You've never heard from your father?"

"Not even a request for money."

Elyssa suddenly thought of the man in her dreams. He— whoever he was—had never tried to contact her, never come searching for her. She'd prayed, for quite a while, that he would. But he never had. That single fact, more than anything else, had shaped her convictions about what she must have done on a Caribbean island called Corazón more than six and a half years before.

"Have you ever looked for him?" she asked.

Alex shrugged. "Why look for someone you don't want to find?"

Their conversation drifted to less personal topics after that.

To her surprise, Elyssa found herself enjoying the meal and the man she was sharing it with. Alex was the most disturbingly complicated individual she'd ever met, but he was capable of being very charming. He had a quick, probing intelligence and a quirky sense of humor that startled her into laughter more than a few times.

He was also extremely attentive.

It was difficult not to feel flattered by the intensity of his interest in her. It was equally difficult not to be flustered by it. Elyssa was not used to being watched as though she'd been put on display in a spotlight on a stage. And she was certainly not used to being made aware of her own physicality—of the caress of her hair against her neck or the shape of her body beneath her clothes.

She kept silent about Alex's scrutiny for a long time, then finally spoke up over dessert. By that time, the stroke of his brown-gold eyes was making it hard for her to keep her hand from trembling as she tried to eat the white chocolate mousse with raspberry sauce she'd ordered.

"Is there something on my nose?" she inquired finally, striving for a lighthearted tone.

Caught up in a contemplation of her mouth, Alex answered without considering the consequences. "Freckles."

"Freckles?" Elyssa's spoon fell from suddenly slack fingers.

He nodded slowly. "About a dozen of them."

Elyssa swallowed. She didn't know why his reply struck her as being such an intimate thing to say. She only knew it did.

"You have very good vision," she observed, shifting uncomfortably.

Alex cocked a brow, his masculine instincts coming to alert as he assessed her obvious uneasiness. Unbidden, his mind flashed back to the lazy, languid afternoon he'd counted and kissed each one of Dawn's freckles.

Not all of those freckles had been on her nose.

Acting on automatic pilot, Elyssa leaned over and retrieved her purse, which she'd placed on the floor by her chair when they'd been seated. Reaching inside, she took out her monogrammed compact and snapped it open.

"There's no reason—" Alex started quickly, then broke off abruptly as he focused on the compact's elegantly engraved cover. Unable to stop himself, he reached across the table and caught Elyssa by the wrist.

She looked at him with startled, sky-colored eyes. "Alex?"

Her skin was very soft against his fingertips. The pounding of her pulse was very rapid. He inclined his head toward the compact.

"E.D.C.?" he asked, tightening his grip as though she might try to escape from him.

The possessive press of the hard male fingers circling her wrist played havoc with Elyssa's ability to think clearly. It took her a few moments to sort out what Alex wanted to know.

"They're my initials," she finally answered. Her voice was huskier than usual, but she couldn't help it. "E.D.C. Elyssa Dawn Collins."

"So..."

"So?"

It was about forty-five minutes later. Elyssa and Alex were facing each other outside the entrance of her Charles Street apartment building. She'd intended to go home alone. He'd insisted on escorting her to her Greenwich Village destination.

Elyssa looked down at the tips of her shoes for a moment, then raised her eyes to Alex's once again. There was a slight nip in the April night air, but she did not feel the least bit cold.

"Thank you for tonight," she said quietly.

"You're welcome," he responded.

Several seconds went by. Elyssa fingered the key to the apartment building.

"Well, ah, good night, Alex."

"Good night."

Alex watched her turn away from him to unlock the building's front door. She dipped her head slightly and her hair swung forward, baring the satiny smooth nape of her neck. He exhaled in a rush as he recalled the meltingly sensual response he'd once drawn by kissing that very sensitive spot.

He couldn't let it end like this. He couldn't!

"Dawn," he said, his voice deep and dark.

Elyssa pivoted back, her cheeks pale, her eyes huge. "What did you say?"

Alex brought his hands up to cup her face, stroking the pads of his thumbs against her skin. "Your name."

"My *middle* name." She shivered as she felt his fingertips tease the lobes of her ears with exquisite care. "I'm not—" She shivered again. "Don't call me that."

"It suits you."

"No."

"Yes."

"Alex—"

He silenced her protest by the simple expedient of bending his head and kissing her as he'd wanted to kiss her since the first moment he'd found her in the Moranco conference room.

Alex fit his mouth over Elyssa's with slow, searing thoroughness. He tunneled through her hair with both hands, cupping the back of her head, controlling the angled offering of her face. He moved his lips against hers with demanding deliberation, searching for the sweetness he'd been deprived of for more than six and a half years.

Elyssa had no defense against the sensual onslaught Alex released within her. A brief impulse to resist was swept away by an overwhelming need to respond. The throb of frustration she'd woken with that morning became a wild clamoring for satiation. She brought her arms up, sliding them around his neck, clinging to and claiming him at the same time. She closed her eyes.

Alex lifted his mouth for just a split second, whispering the name by which he'd first known the woman now trembling in his arms. Then, with a groan, he began kissing her again, even more passionately than before.

Elyssa opened her lips to him, welcoming the velvet glide of his tongue over hers. The taste of him flooded her. She felt his strong hands sweep down the length of her back and come to rest, splay-fingered, at the base of her spine. He pressed her tight against him. She surged up on tiptoe, wanting to get closer, then closer still.

It was like her dream, but without the storm, and she wanted it to go on and on and on....

Alex had initiated the kiss. Drawing on every shred of self-control he possessed, he finally brought it to an end. He didn't want to, but he knew they were careening toward a point they had no business reaching on a public sidewalk.

"Open your eyes," he said hoarsely, his breath coming in short, shallow gasps. You know, he thought with a fierce sense of triumph. I *know* you know me!

He watched Elyssa sway uncertainly, then do as he'd bidden. Her eyelids fluttered open. She stared at him blindly. Blankly. Bewilderedly.

"Alex?" she asked.

He saw a hunger as great as his own in her eyes.

He saw even more questions than he had glimpsed that afternoon.

But he still saw no hint of recognition.

Three

Elyssa was not in the best of moods when she stepped off the elevator into Carradine and Associates' elegant reception area about three-thirty the following afternoon.

She'd gotten very little sleep the night before and had woken up feeling both unsettled and exhausted. Her prescription for dealing with this situation—a freezing cold shower and three cups of black coffee—had left her covered with goosebumps and wired on caffeine.

Next she'd had to contend with an uncharacteristic eruption of brattiness from her daughter. It had begun with Sandy whining about not being allowed to eat cookies for breakfast and had climaxed with her shrilly declaring that kindergarten was stinky, that the sitter who took care of her each day after school was stupid, and that her mommy was mean, mean, mean. Elyssa's prescription for responding to this tantrum—a sincere effort to be patient punctuated by a swift swatting of her little girl's derriere—had left her emotionally drained.

Then she'd had to go to work, where her assignment for the day had been to accompany one of the firm's most creative but least organized associates on a shopping expedition for a client and take notes. Her prescription for coping in this case—do her job and prevent the absentminded associate from stepping off the curb into oncoming traffic—had left her with eyestrain, writer's cramp, and sore feet.

The last thing Elyssa needed when she returned to her workplace was to have Nikki Spears swoop down on her the instant she set foot in the reception area. Given her friend's all-black outfit of the day, it was a bit like being attacked by a bat.

"Where have you been, Lys?" the brunette cried.

Concerned by Nikki's manner, Elyssa immediately thought of her daughter. The skin on the back of her neck tightened.

"Is something wrong?" she asked quickly, a rush of anxiety overwhelming her weariness.

"Wrong?"

"Is it Sandy?"

The brunette looked blank for a moment. Then, "Oh! Oh, no. She's fine. At least, as far as I know, she's fine."

"Then what—?"

Nikki clutched Elyssa's arm. "You've *got* to see what's sitting on your desk."

"My...desk?"

"Come on, Lys."

Elyssa was too tired to resist. She allowed herself to be dragged off to her work cubicle. She was dimly aware that her progress seemed to stir an unusual amount of interest in her co-workers.

"So, what do you have to say about *this?*" Nikki demanded once they'd reached their destination. She let go of Elyssa's arm in order to make the kind of flourishing gesture normally performed only by game show models.

Elyssa caught her breath.

The "this" was a crystal vase filled with a dozen sprays of orchids. There were four or five small, exquisitely formed blossoms on each stem. The frilled edges of the creamy petals were a delicate blush pink. The throats of the flowers were a deeper, much more provocative hue.

"Oh..." she breathed as she tried to absorb the astonishing loveliness of the utterly unexpected offering. She stepped forward slowly, moving like a sleepwalker.

She had seen orchids like these before. Somewhere. Sometime.

Elyssa reached out and touched one of the flowers. She traced its ruffled edges, then lightly stroked the silken surfaces of its petals. After a few seconds, she lifted her fingers to her nose. The scent that lingered on her skin was as elusive as it was exotic.

Somewhere...

Sometime...

"'Oh'?" Nikki echoed. "That's all you have to say is 'oh'?"

Elyssa made no response, her attention still focused on the beautiful bouquet. There was a small white envelope nestled among the sprays of orchids. She plucked it out, opened it, and extracted the pasteboard rectangle. The name "Alex"—nothing more—was written on the card in an angular scrawl.

Elyssa's heart turned over in her breast. She pressed her flower-scented fingers against her lips as the memory of the kiss she had received and responded to the night before came flooding back. She once again felt the hot, hungry search of Alex's mouth. The tips of her breasts tightened. Something deep inside her trembled.

This isn't me, she thought. I'm not like this!

"From Alexander Moran?" Nikki asked in an odd voice.

Elyssa felt the weight of her friend's gaze, but she didn't turn her head. "Yes," she affirmed.

Alexander Moran.

Elyssa repeated the name silently. Why had this man, of all the men she'd met in the past six and a half years, had such an immediate and intense effect upon her? she wondered. What was there about him that stirred emotions she hadn't even realized she possessed? How, in the space of a single day, had he managed to unsettle the foundations of the life she'd so carefully built since coming to New York?

A single public meeting with him had left her feeling as though lightning had struck somewhere nearby. Their eyes had met, their hands had touched, and the air around them had seemed to quiver with electricity.

The meal they'd shared had only served to heighten her responses. She'd felt linked to him, as though they'd been bonded by some invisible and irresistible force.

And then, dear heaven, he'd kissed her! He'd kissed her and she'd gone up in flames. If Alex hadn't lifted his mouth from hers when he did, she didn't know how far she would have—

"Lys?"

Elyssa came back to the present with a start. She looked at Nikki questioningly but didn't speak.

"There's a message on your phone," the brunette informed her.

Elyssa shifted her eyes instantly. There was, indeed, a pink message slip stuck to the receiver of her phone.

"Mr. Moran of Moranco called at 9:33 a.m.," it read. "Please call back." A seven-digit number followed.

No *wonder* her return to her desk had merited so much attention from her colleagues! Elyssa thought. When the client responsible for what Nikki had accurately described as Carradine and Associates' biggest commercial contract of the year called one of the firm's lower-ranking employees, it was bound to stir a fair amount of speculation.

"Are you going to?" Nikki asked.

"Going to what?"

"Call him back."

Elyssa hesitated, caught in a welter of contradictory emotions. She wanted to speak to Alexander Moran again. She wanted to see him again, too. She couldn't deny it. She was fascinated by him. But, at the same time, she was frightened by that fascination.

So, what should she do? Turn her back on the emotions Alex evoked in her? Deny they were real? Run away from them?

No! she decided. She'd tried running from reality once. In fact, some might say she'd done so twice. Once when she'd flown to an island called Corazón, trying to escape the bitter proof of her failure as a woman. The second time when she'd fled her home and family for New York. She couldn't—wouldn't—do it again.

"Yes," she told Nikki quietly. "I'm going to call him."

"Are you sure that's such a good idea?"

"I have to thank him for the flowers, Nikki."

"How about writing him a nice note instead?"

"For heaven's sake! *You're* the one who wanted me to go out with him."

Nikki sighed heavily. "I know. I know. You don't have to remind me. This is all my fault."

"*Your* fault? How can you say—"

"I saw the way you looked when you came home last night, Lys," Nikki cut in bluntly.

Elyssa started to raise a hand to her mouth. She realized what she was doing and stopped. There was nothing she could do to halt the telltale rush of blood up into her face.

"How did I look, Nikki?" she asked.

Nikki grimaced. "You looked ravished," she said, then gestured with a hint of exasperation. "Or maybe I mean ravishing. Maybe both. Ravished *and* ravishing. Oh, I don't know! You just didn't look like you, Lys! And it was obviously because of him. Alexander Moran. It—well, frankly, it scared me a little."

Elyssa moistened her lips with the tip of her tongue. "It scared me a little, too," she admitted after a few moments.

"But you're still going to call him."

"Yes."

"Lys—"

"I have to, Nikki."

The brunette shook her head. "I hope you know what you're doing."

Elyssa managed a crooked smile. "So do I."

Brrr-iing. Brrr-iing.

"Good afternoon. Mr. Moran's office."

"Good afternoon. This is Elyssa Collins returning Mr. Moran's call. Is he in, please?"

"Elys—oh! Oh, *yes,* Mrs. Collins. He's in. Just one moment."

Click.

Elyssa nibbled her lower lip, trying to ignore the fluttering in her stomach. She reached out and brushed her fingertips against one of the orchids.

Mrs. Collins, she echoed silently. She wished the lie about her widowhood hadn't been necessary. Unfortunately she'd started telling it more than six years ago and it was now accepted as "the truth" by everyone she knew in New York. Well, almost everyone. She continued to suspect that Nikki was highly skeptical of the story. Nonetheless she'd told the lie to others, so she'd had to tell it to Alex. She'd had no choice!

Elyssa withdrew her hand from the flower she'd been touching.

Click.

"Elyssa?"

"Yes, Alex," Elyssa responded. "I'm sorry it's taken me so long to return your call."

"That's all right. I'm just glad you did."

"You thought I might not?"

There was a strained silence.

"After last night—" Alex began, his voice several notes lower than it had been.

"Last night was last night," Elyssa interrupted quickly, straightening in her chair. Although she knew Nikki had left the work cubicle, she darted a quick glance over her shoulder to make absolutely certain she was alone. There was no point in providing any more grist for the office gossip mill. "This is today, and today I want to thank you for the flowers you sent me."

"You liked them, then." The words were more assertion than inquiry, and they were edged with an emotion Elyssa couldn't identify.

"How could I not?" she returned. "They're beautiful. I've never—"

She stopped, a sense of déjà vu nibbling once again at the edge of her consciousness. She couldn't say she'd never seen orchids like the ones he'd sent because she had the definite impression that she had. She just didn't know where or when.

"Elyssa?"

Elyssa shook her head, trying to clear it. "The flowers are breathtaking, Alex. Thank you."

"You're welcome."

There was another pause in the conversation. Elyssa crossed her legs.

"Was there a reason you called me?" she asked finally.

"Oh, yes," Alex responded in a dark velvet tone. As she had the evening before, Elyssa sensed deep and double meanings in his reply. "I have tickets for a show on Friday." He named a recently opened Broadway musical which reportedly was sold out for at least a year. "Would you come with me?"

Elyssa went to the theater with Alex on Friday and had dinner with him on the following Tuesday. Two days after that, her path crossed his in the gutted and gloomy lobby of the hotel he'd hired Carradine and Associates to refurbish.

Each time she saw him—spent time with him—her attraction to him grew. But so did her anxiety about that attraction. She found herself thinking about moths and flames. There was light and warmth in Alex Moran, but she also sensed there was the capacity to burn...and burn badly.

There was no repetition of the kiss he had given her at the end of their first evening together. Elyssa was thankful for this. It was not that she didn't long to feel the press of his mouth against hers again. She did. The thought of it made her brain haze and her body hum. But the potency of her response—even after the fact—was very disturbing to her. For all the connection she felt with him, Alexander Moran was still essentially a stranger to her.

The night after the day she'd seen Alex at the hotel site, there was a storm.

If she had the dream that night, Elyssa did not remember it.

Alex paced the living room of his Central Park co-op apartment restlessly.

He still didn't know what to think. Dawn—Elyssa—didn't remember him. Or, if she did, she was concealing it with a skill that would put a host of Academy Award-winning performers to shame. Either way, he was left feeling frustrated and furious.

What he'd endured during the past eleven days was like being torn apart *and* tied into knots. He couldn't eat. Couldn't sleep. Could barely keep his mind on business. When he wasn't with Elyssa, he wanted to be and when he was...

God! How could he describe the emotions that stormed through him when they were together? One moment he wanted to stroke her. The next moment he wanted to strangle her! There were times when he was almost overwhelmed by the urge to shake her. To shout at her. To demand she tell him the truth!

And there were other times when it took every bit of self-discipline he had not to take her into his arms and kiss her and caress her until she moaned and melted. "The truth"—whatever that was—didn't seem to matter much at those times.

Alex stopped pacing, breathing hard and fast, trying to ignore the all-too-familiar feeling of heaviness between this thighs. He ran both hands back through his hair several times. His fingers were not completely steady.

"What am I going to do?" he asked aloud.

He'd thought about turning his back on her. About cutting his losses, as it were. But how could he? The "loss" he'd cut if he walked away now would be his heart.

He might have been able to do it if Dawn had changed in some essential way during the past six and a half years. He didn't mean change physically. There was no denying that it had been the beauty of her face and body that had first drawn him to her. But it had been her spirit...her soul...that had held him. She still possessed all the qualities that had captivated him on Isla de la Corazón. She possessed all of them and more!

She—Dawn—had been half-girl.

She—Elyssa—was all woman. There was a strength about her that he found seductive in the extreme.

Alex resumed his pacing.

He'd considered confronting her, of course. He'd been on the brink of asking hard questions and demanding honest answers more times than he could count since the meeting in the Moranco conference room. But something he couldn't—or wouldn't—name had held him back from doing so.

He'd considered confiding in Philip Lassiter and asking his help in ferreting out the truth, too. He'd reached for the phone over and over again, intending to do just that. Pride had kept him from actually picking up the receiver and dialing.

How in the name of heaven could he tell his friend that the woman whose memory he'd clung to for more than six and a half years didn't recall him at all? Or, if she did, that she wouldn't admit it? *How could he do that?*

Alex swore, clenching his hands into fists.

He knew how Philip would react if he did tell him. Philip would say and do all the right things. He always did. He would rationalize and sympathize. He would offer kindness and comfort. But, underneath, Philip would be pitying him. His friend and lawyer would be pitying him for being a fool.

Pity was an emotion Alex had never sought, would never accept, simply could not endure.

He suddenly felt stifled. Closed in. Crossing the living room, he pushed open the sliding glass door that led to the terrace of his twentieth floor apartment and walked out into the sunshine.

Alex leaned against the terrace railing, dimly registering that it was still damp from the heavy rain that had fallen the night before. He stared out at the city.

Elyssa Dawn Collins.

He wanted her. He wanted her in every way a man could want a woman. He wanted her more now than he'd wanted her six and half years before on Isla de la Corazón.

He'd told Dawn in the heat of passion that he needed her. He hadn't realized how deeply this need ran until he'd lost her. She'd become a vital part of him during their time together. Without her, he was incomplete.

Alex lowered his head for a moment, swallowing hard. He closed his eyes. He felt an errant April breeze ruffle his hair and finger his cheek. He heard the honking of a dozen different cars from the street far below.

It was more than wanting and he knew it. He loved her. Despite everything else, he loved her. It was as simple—and as complicated—as that.

About an hour later, Alex stood in front of the security intercom at Elyssa's apartment building. His finger was fixed on the button next to the label that read "E. Collins."

Buzzzzzzzzz.

No answer. He eased the pressure on the button for just an instant then applied it once again.

Buzzzzzzzzz!

"Mister, are you looking for somebody?"

Alex controlled a jerk of surprise, then pivoted away from the intercom board. He found himself facing a pair of trendily dressed preteen girls. One was a slightly pudgy redhead with glasses. The other was a spaghetti-thin black with braces. Both of them were studying him with a mixture of curiosity and caution.

"Yes," he confirmed. "I'm looking for Elyssa Collins."

The black girl wrinkled her nose. "She not here right now."

Alex's mouth twisted. "So I gathered. I've been buzzing her apartment." He paused for a beat. "Do you know where she is?"

The two girls exchanged glances, then resumed their scrutiny of him.

"I'm a friend of Mrs. Collins," Alex added, hoping this might help tip the scales in his favor.

The girls looked at each other silently once again, apparently communicating by some form of adolescent ESP. After a few seconds, they nodded simultaneously. When they turned their attention back to him, their expressions were much more approving.

"Elyssa's probably at the park," the black girl informed him. "She usually is, this time on Saturdays."

"The park?"

"Abingdon Square Park," the redhead specified, speaking up for the first time. "You know. At Hudson and Bleeker."

Actually, Alex did not know. But he certainly intended to find out.

"Thank you," he said to the girls and smiled.

The girls traded wide-eyed looks, then burst into self-conscious giggles.

Alex expected Abingdon Square Park to be like the Village's famous Washington Square Park: a three-ring circus showcasing some of the best—and worst—contemporary New York City had to offer. While what he found was hardly a serene and sylvan refuge, the hustle and bustle seemed very wholesome.

He spotted Elyssa easily and felt an instant quickening of his pulse when he did. She was standing by herself, shading her eyes with one hand, her attention fixed on a group of young children playing tag. She was smiling.

Her clothes were quite a departure from the quietly chic garments she'd had on the last five times he'd seen her. Today she was dressed very casually—sneakers, a pair of snug-fitting jeans, and a roomy, hot-pink pullover. Her hair was different too. Instead of being carefully smoothed into a classic pageboy, it was tousled about her face.

Alex walked toward her swiftly, eating up the distance between them in long, hungry strides. The last time he'd moved as quickly had been six and a half years before, when he'd seen a slender, sun-gilded blonde on a white sand beach on a Caribbean island called Corazón.

Elyssa laughed happily as she watched her daughter chase a friend around a small patch of the park. Such energy! Such determination! When she remembered how frighteningly fragile Sandy had been at birth, the glowing good health her little girl now possessed seemed like a miracle.

Sandy was small for her age, true. But she was also strong and quick and very, very bright.

Whomever Sandy's father had been, Elyssa thought with a pang, he had certainly helped create a remarkable child.

A sudden quiver of awareness ran through her. Turning away from the game of tag, she found herself face-to-face with Alex Moran.

Elyssa asked herself later what had prompted her to pivot so abruptly. Had she heard him approach? Had she caught a glimpse of him out of the corner of her eyes? Or…had she somehow *sensed* his nearness?

"Alex!" she exclaimed.

Elyssa's abrupt turn caught Alex by surprise. He took a moment to recover, ruthlessly clamping down on the surge of desire that coursed through him like molten metal as he looked down into her wide blue eyes.

"Hello, Elyssa," he said finally. He saw her cheeks grow pink and wondered how much of what he was feeling showed in his face.

"What are you doing here?" Elyssa asked, trying to absorb the possible implications of Alex's unexpected appearance. She found herself more conscious than she'd ever been of his size. His casual attire—battered athletic shoes, well-worn black cord slacks, a white T-shirt, and an ancient black leather jacket—underscored the power of his physical presence in a very unsettling way.

"Would you believe I just happened to be in the neighborhood?" Alex countered wryly.

Elyssa pretended to ponder this explanation for a few seconds, then tilted her head to one side. "No, I don't think so."

A sudden breeze sent a glossy lock of hair fluttering across her face. Unable to stop himself, Alex reached out and stroked it back behind her ear. He felt her tremble for an instant as his fingertips brushed against her fine-grained skin.

"I'm here because I wanted to see you again," he said with devastating candor. "I need—"

Alex never got an opportunity to finish his sentence. He was interrupted by the whirlwind appearance of a pixie-pretty little girl with long brown braids.

"Mommy! Mommy!" The child was almost incandescent with glee. "Did you see me? I winned!"

Alex froze, impaled on a simple, two-syllable word. He couldn't move. He couldn't speak.

Mommy.

Dear God. Was this little girl Dawn's *daughter?*

"You won, sweetie? That's terrific." Elyssa bent to give Sandy a hug. She caught a glimpse of Alex's angular face as she did so. The expression she saw made her heart do a somersault. He looked furious.

Oh, no, she thought. *Not like this. I never intended him to find out about Sandy like this!*

Elyssa wasn't certain why she hadn't told Alex about her daughter. Sandy was, after all, one of her favorite topics of conversation. Yet, with Alexander Moran, she'd obeyed an instinct that had warned her to say nothing about the most precious person in her life.

Perhaps she'd kept quiet because he seemed to take so little of what she told him about herself at surface value. He paid attention to every single word she said, and he asked frighteningly perceptive questions after he did so. It was one thing for Nikki Spears to have doubts about her story. It would be entirely another if this man did.

Elyssa wasn't ashamed of Sandy. Her mother and stepfather were, but she wasn't. Yet she *was* ashamed of the circumstances of Sandy's conception. Or, to be more accurate, she was ashamed of what she believed those circumstances must have been.

Alex recovered his capacity to speak and move. "I didn't realize you had a daughter," he said tightly, staring down at mother and child. He'd reconciled himself, just barely, to the idea that she'd pledged herself to another man in marriage. But the thought that she'd borne that man's child, too, was like a knife to his heart.

Elyssa straightened but still kept a hand resting protectively on one of Sandy's small shoulders. "Yes. I know," she answered, wondering if her voice sounded as quavery to him as it did to her. "I'm sorry—"

At that moment, Sandy did an astonishing thing.

"My name is Sandy," she piped up, shrugging off her mother's hand and taking a step toward Alex. Tilting her head back, she favored him with a beaming smile. "What's your name?"

Elyssa caught her breath. She'd never seen Sandy take this kind of initiative with a stranger. While her daughter was not shy, she was normally very wary around people she didn't know. Especially when those people were male.

"My name is Alex," Alex answered after a moment. Although the little girl's coloring was darker, he could see a great deal of Elyssa in her. He wondered if that was why, despite the emotional turmoil he was experiencing, he found it impossible not to respond to Sandy's smile. "Alex Moran."

Sandy's delicate features crumpled together in concentration for a few seconds, then smoothed out. "I know you," she announced in a tone of great satisfaction. "You're the man Aunt Nikki talked about!"

"Sandy!" Elyssa gasped.

"Aunt Nikki?" Alex questioned at the same time.

Sandy blithely ignored her mother. She bobbed her head up and down, making her braids bounce. "Aunt Nikki is my mommy's friend. She's not really truly my aunt, but she says it's okay if I called her that. Her favorite color for clothes is black. You know why?"

"I'm afraid not," Alex admitted.

"Because black is basic." Sandy offered this pronouncement with the aplomb of the editor-in-chief of the world's most elegant fashion magazine.

"I see." Without even thinking about what he was doing, Alex hunkered down to the little girl's level. "That's very interesting."

"I know lots of int'resting stuff," Sandy boasted, then itched her pert, freckle-dusted nose. "Are you my mommy's friend, too? Like Aunt Nikki?"

"Well, not exactly like Aunt Nikki."

"Because you're a man and she's a lady?"

"Ah . . . something like that."

Alex glanced up at Elyssa. While he was still very angry that she'd failed to tell him she had a daughter, he was finding it difficult to hang on to his fury in the face of Sandy's artless charm. Perhaps all youngsters had her innocent appeal. He didn't know. His experience with children was almost nil. Then again, perhaps this little girl was special.

Elyssa evaded Alex's gaze. "Sandy," she said firmly, "it's not polite to ask so many questions."

Sandy turned her head. "Why not?"

Elyssa later told herself she should have been prepared for that one. Unfortunately the inquiry caught her by surprise. "Well . . . well, because—"

Sandy turned back to Alex. "Does it make you mad when I ask questions?"

Alex's mouth twisted. "Not at all, Sandy. I like questions." The answer was for the daughter, the inflection for the mother. Out of the corner of his eye, he saw Elyssa stiffen and knew his barb had found its mark.

Obviously pleased, Sandy took him at his word. "Do you have a job?"

"Mmm-hmm."

"What kind of job?"

"Well, I sometimes build buildings."

"I build things, too!" Sandy exclaimed excitedly. "With my blocks."

"I guess we have something in common, then."

"What's 'in common'?"

Alex puzzled over this for a moment. It seemed strangely important to him to explain the phrase properly. "It means we both like the same thing, Sandy," he said finally.

"Oh." Sandy nibbled on her lower lips, then asked. "Do you like burgers and fries?"

"Absolutely," Alex assured her. "Do you?"

"Uh-huh." Sandy nodded vehemently. "Mommy likes them, too. Does that mean we're all in common?"

"Sounds like it to me."

Elyssa knew what was coming before her daughter turned around and looked at her with hopeful brown eyes.

"Mommy," Sandy began in a wheedling tone, "can Mr. M'ran have lunch with us?"

The lunch, at a nearby fast-food place, was almost as disorienting to Elyssa as the first dinner she'd shared with Alex. It was not so much that she had a sense of dangerous emotional currents eddying beneath the surface of the encounter—although she did, indeed, have that sense. It was more a matter of feeling she was witnessing a facet of Alexander Moran's personality that was unfamiliar even to him.

To put it simply, his manner toward Sandy was as astonishing as hers toward him. He teased her, but he never talked down to her. He also proved to be extraordinarily patient in the face of an endless stream of curious inquiries.

Only once during the meal did he seem to pull back. That was when Sandy informed him she didn't have a daddy because he'd gone to heaven before she was "borned." Elyssa, who would have found the topic of her daughter's father disturbing under any circumstances, quickly changed subjects. After a few silent minutes, Alex rejoined the conversation.

Following lunch, the three of them went for a stroll. Sandy positioned herself between the two adults, skipping and chattering. Her mood was as sunny as the day's weather. Elyssa found herself looking over her daughter's head and exchanging smiles with Alex. She felt more at ease with him than ever before.

And then something peculiar happened.

Sandy was merrily discussing her favorite fairy tale when she suddenly broke off and gazed longingly into a shop window. "That's what I really, really *really* want for my birthday," she announced.

"You have a birthday coming up?" Alex asked.

"Uh-huh. On tomorrow."

"Tomorrow?"

"Yeah. Mommy's making me a party. Guess how old I'm going to be."

Elyssa watched Alex assess her daughter intently. Most people underestimated Sandy's age because of her size.

"Forty-three?" he eventually suggested, the expression in his eyes contradicting the joking tone in his voice.

Sandy giggled. "No, you silly. Six!" She held up the appropriate number of fingers to emphasize the information.

Alex said nothing—then. But a short time later, he offered some very perfunctory excuses and left them.

Sandy was bereft.

Elyssa was bewildered.

Alex sat on the low-slung leather sofa in his living room, staring at the tattered photograph he'd placed on the coffee table in front of him. To the right of the snapshot was an untouched glass of Scotch. To the left was a telephone, also untouched.

Six.

He repeated the number silently. Sandy Collins was going to be six years old tomorrow, April the twenty-fourth.

He and Dawn had first made love on September the twenty-second, six years and seven months before.

Dear God. Had they also made a child? It was possible. He knew more than enough about the facts of life to know it *was* possible.

I'm a widow, Elyssa had said.

My daddy went to heaven before I was borned, her daughter had told him.

Had Elyssa been married when they'd come together on Isla de la Corazón? Had what had been a life-altering experience for him been only an adulterous fling for her? Was that why she didn't remember him?

Had she been pregnant with her husband's child when they'd made love? Basic human biology said that was possible, too. Probable, in fact.

Alex's stomach roiled.

He'd known he hadn't been Dawn's first lover. She'd been with at least one man before him. Nonetheless there'd been an awkwardness about her physical responses that had made him believe her previous sexual experience was extremely limited. Unless she'd been a better actress than any woman he'd ever encountered, she'd been genuinely stunned by the intensity of the pleasure their joining had given her.

She hadn't been a virgin. But she *had* been an innocent. Or so he'd thought for more than six and a half years.

Now he didn't know what to think.

He had to find out the truth! He had to discover who Elyssa Dawn Collins was, what had happened to her, and whether or not she'd had his—*his!*—child.

Alex picked up the phone and punched out a number.

One ring.

Two rings.

"Hello?"

"Philip, this is Alex. I want you to contact the investigation agency. I need to know everything there is to know about a woman called Elyssa Collins."

"What?"

Alex repeated his order.

"But—"

"She's twenty-seven," Alex plowed ahead. "She was born somewhere near Chicago. She works for Carradine and Associates. She's a widow and she has a six-year-old daughter named Sandy."

There was a tense silence. Alex heard Philip give a long, drawn-out sigh.

"Alex," the lawyer began in an extremely cautious tone, "Alex, who is this woman?"

"That's what I'm trying to find out."

"I don't understand."

Alex touched the photograph on the coffee table with the tip of his finger. Then, very quietly, he said, "She's Dawn, Philip. Elyssa Collins is Dawn, but she doesn't remember me."

Four

Alex fully intended to stay away from Elyssa until the investigation he'd ordered done on her was completed. At least, that's what he told himself after he'd said goodbye to Philip.

I'll get the facts, then I'll face her.

He told himself the same thing on Sandy's sixth birthday.

He told it to himself again the following day.

And the day after that.

On Wednesday evening, Alex's resolve broke and he phoned Elyssa from his apartment. Just to speak to her, he vowed.

One ring.

Two rings.

Three—

"H'llo?"

Alex almost hung up. The treble voice on the other end of the line was immediately recognizable, if a trifle muffled.

"Sandy?" he asked after a moment.

"Uh-huh."

"This is Alex Moran."

"Oh, hi, Mr. M'ran!" This enthusiastic greeting was followed by a brief pause. Alex heard what sounded like chewing and swallowing. "I had banana in my mouth," Sandy explained artlessly when she spoke again. "What are you doing?"

Alex forked a hand back through his hair. What the hell *was* he doing? he wondered grimly.

"Well, what I'm doing right now is talking to you on the phone, Sandy," he responded carefully keeping his voice gentle.

The little girl giggled delightedly at this answer.

"Is your mother there?"

"Uh-huh. She's in the bathroom. Do you want me to tell her she should hurry up?"

"No, that's all right," Alex refused. "I'll wait."

"And talk to me?" Sandy asked hopefully.

"And talk to you." He paused, his chest tightening. What if this little girl was his child? What if Dawn—*Elyssa*—had borne his baby yet pretended it was her husband's? What if—God! Did she even know who Sandy's father was?

One thing was certain. Elyssa Dawn Collins cared for her daughter. Alex had seen the softness in her face when she looked at Sandy, heard the tenderness in her voice when she talked to the little girl. Maternity became her like candlelight—it made her glow.

"Mr. M'ran?"

Alex raked his fingers through his hair again. "Yes, Sandy?"

"You want to talk about my birthday party?"

Under different circumstances, Alex probably would have chuckled at the little girl's wheedling tone. Unfortunately he had not felt like laughing for more than four days.

"Good idea," he answered. "How was it?"

"Really great! Everybody I 'vited came. Mommy hanged pink b'loons and shiny streamers and made up all these fun games where everybody winned a prize. After we played, I opened my presents. Aunt Nikki—she was there, too—said I raked in the loot. That means I got lots of good stuff. You should see, Mr. M'ran. I even got a play kitchen. It was just like the one I showed you, 'member?''

"Yes, I remember." Sweet heaven, how he remembered!

"The only bad thing was my friend, Dina," Sandy chattered on. "She ate too much cake and ice cream and threw up. It was kind of yucky and I thought Mommy would get mad but she didn't. Dina's okay now. She hit Kevin Clancy at school today 'cuz he said he wouldn't be her boyfriend. She got in trouble with the teacher. You know, I think having boyfriends is dumb. I'm never going to have one. Not even when I'm old as—oh! *Oh!* Guess what?"

Alex had absolutely no idea "what" and he said as much.

"I'm going on a trip on Saturday!" Sandy informed him breathlessly. "To Connecticut. Do you know where that is? My friend Michelle's gran'ma and gran'pa live there. They have a house with a swimming pool and ponies! Michelle asked me did I want to visit there with her and I said yes. Then her mommy asked my mommy to be sure, and my mommy said yes, too! This will be the first time I ever went away by myself. But I'm not scared. Only babies are scared. And I'm not—" She broke off abruptly. "Oh-oh. Here's mommy. Bye, Mr. M'ran."

"Goodbye, Sandy," Alex replied. He heard some type of exchange between mother and daughter but couldn't make out the words. His mouth went dry. His stomach felt hollow.

"Alex?" Elyssa's voice was tentative.

"Hello, Elyssa."

"How have you been?"

She's noticed I haven't called, he decided instantly. She's noticed and she's wondered why. But is that because of a guilty conscience or because she missed me?

"I've been busy," he said aloud.

"I see."

"And you?"

"Oh, I've been busy, too."

There was a break in the conversation then. Alex drummed his fingers against his thigh. He could imagine Elyssa nibbling on her lower lip or twisting a lock of hair around her fingers. After about ten seconds, he heard her take a deep breath, as though she was steeling herself to say something important. He waited, his entire body tense, but she remained silent.

"Elyssa?" he prompted finally.

She cleared her throat. "I was just wondering why you'd called."

Alex almost told her then and there. The truth trembled on the tip of his tongue, burning like acid.

Why did I call? he wanted to say. *I called because I needed to hear your voice again so badly I ached. I called because every scenario I've thought of to explain you and Sandy and Isla de la Corazón is an ugly one and ugly doesn't fit you! I called because I have to understand who you are and what's happened!*

Alex choked back the words. This was not the time for them. He would confront her when he had the facts. When he could deal with whatever was going on between them by relying on information—not by reacting to emotion.

"No special reason," he answered evenly. "I hadn't spoken to you in a few days and I wanted to talk for a few minutes. Do you mind?"

"No!" came the quick, from-the-core assurance. It was followed by a self-conscious little laugh. Then, in a more moderate tone, Elyssa said, "No. Of course I don't mind, Alex. I . . . I'm glad you called."

She sounded so sincere. And the hint of shyness in her speech suggested that "glad" was a substitute for a much stronger adjective, a much warmer emotion. But, dammit! How could he reconcile this apparent sincerity and shyness with all the other things he knew about her?

"I'm glad you're glad," Alex returned, clenching and unclenching his free hand. "I, ah, understand you're going to be alone this weekend."

"Alone?" she echoed warily. "I don't—oh. Sandy told you about her trip to Connecticut."

"To the house with the pool and the ponies."

"That's the one."

He heard a trace of uneasiness in her voice. "Are you worried about her going away without you?"

Elyssa sighed. "No. Not exactly. The family she's going
with is wonderful. It's just that—well, Sandy's very anxious to be what she calls a 'big girl.' But I don't want her to
rush things. I mean, it seems like only yesterday I was cradling her in my arms at the hospital and now she's six! She'll
be in first grade next fall. She's growing up so quickly.
Sometimes I'm afraid it's *too* quickly."

"Well, at least you don't have to be concerned about
boyfriends yet."

"What?"

"Sandy told me she thinks having boyfriends is dumb."

"Oh." Elyssa seemed taken aback by this. "It sounds as
though Sandy's told you a great many things."

More than you have, Alex thought. Aloud, he said, "We
had a good talk."

"She doesn't usually take to new people the way she's
taken to you."

"Does it bother you that she has?"

"Bother me? No. No, of course not. It's just that she
tends to be very cautious with strangers."

"That's not necessarily a bad thing in this day and age."

"I realize that." Her words were tinged with sadness, as
though she regretted the conditions that made it necessary
for the innocent to be on guard all the time.

"It must be very difficult raising a child alone," Alex
commented after a few seconds.

"It can be," Elyssa conceded softly. "But having a
healthy, happy little girl makes all the difficulties worth-
while. Believe me."

There was another short pause. Alex fought a brief bat-
tle to put down an idea that had started forming in his brain
as soon as Sandy had mentioned her trip. The idea won.

"Look, Elyssa," he said, "since you're going to be on
your own, will you have dinner with me Saturday night?"
He waited a moment, then added impulsively, "At my
place. I'll cook."

"You cook?"

The mix of skepticism and surprise in her question made
one corner of Alex's mouth kick up. "On rare occasions."

"I see."

"Does that put you off?"

"Not necessarily."

"Is that a yes or a no?"

It was a yes.

The sky was a clear and brilliant blue when Elyssa kissed Sandy goodbye on Saturday morning, but it began to cloud over within a few hours. Rain started falling as she prepared for her dinner date with Alex—lightly at first, then more and more heavily. Gentle April showers had become a driving downpour by the time she arrived at his door.

"Wet?" he asked as he relieved her of her dripping umbrella.

"It's wonderful weather for ducks out there," Elyssa acknowledged with a grimace, then began unbuttoning her raincoat.

"Here, let me," Alex volunteered, moving around behind her. She had her hair pinned up, and the sight of her bared nape affected him as potently as it had eleven nights before, when she'd turned away from him at the front door of her apartment building.

Elyssa gave him a quick smile. "Thank you."

Alex was aware that he let his hands linger a second or two longer than necessary on Elyssa's shoulders and arms as he helped her take off the coat. The temptation to keep on touching her was very strong, but he resisted it. He'd imposed certain limits on himself this evening, and he was going to abide by them.

"We seem to be having a stormy spring this year," he observed neutrally, his eyes running over her. She was wearing a long-sleeved wrap-style dress. The bodice was gently draped, the waist snugly tied. The skirt hinted at the curving lines of her hips rather than hugging them. The heathery rose color of the garment underscored the shimmering fairness of her hair and the translucence of her skin. A single strand of pearls called attention to the slender elegance of her throat.

"So I've noticed," Elyssa replied. Alex's nearness had triggered a quiver of response within her. She smoothed her palms against the soft fabric of her dress, trying to hide her reaction.

"Why don't you go in and make yourself comfortable," Alex suggested after a moment, nodding down the hall. "I'll join you as soon as I hang up your things."

"All right."

Elyssa couldn't deny that the large living room Alex had sent her into was impressive. One wall was virtually all glass, including a set of sliding doors that led out onto a terrace. The view of the city it offered—even on this stormy night—was extremely compelling.

The rest of the decor was equally striking, all ivory creams and charcoal grays with a few shots of jet black. Glass, metal, polished stone, and leather were the dominant materials used. There was no clutter. Nothing that even remotely merited the adjective "cozy." Everything was sleek and spare and immaculately modern.

Yet, as visually stunning as the room was, it seemed oddly impersonal. Elyssa could picture Alex in the austerely elegant setting if she tried, but the image she conjured up was curiously flat. It lacked the unique, multidimensional force of his personality.

The "ruthless" Alexander Moran would fit here, she decided a bit uneasily. The Alexander Moran who made money and did deals without stopping to ask himself "Why?" would be at home—if home were the right word—here, too.

But what about the Alexander Moran who'd kissed her until she was dazed and dizzy? What about the man who'd courted her with exotic flowers and captivated her little daughter? Where was his imprint?

"Would you like some wine?"

Elyssa started guiltily, then turned. Alex was standing a few feet away from her. He had a glass of wine in each hand. Something about his posture made her think he'd been studying her studying his living room for more than a few seconds.

"Oh . . . yes, please."

Alex closed the distance between them in two lithe strides and handed her one of the glasses he was holding. His fingers touched Elyssa's for an instant, and he felt a sizzle of electricity. He saw her eyes widen and knew she must have felt it, too.

He took a quick drink of wine. Elyssa did the same.

"Shall we sit down?" he asked.

"Of course," she agreed.

They moved to the long, low-slung leather sofa that was set against the wall to the right of where they were standing. There was a glass-topped table in front of it, set with an artistically arranged platter of fresh vegetables, two small bowls with dipping sauces, and a stack of plain white napkins.

"Have you lived here long?" Elyssa inquired, seating herself. Alex sat down a moment later, leaving perhaps two feet between them. While he was far enough away so she didn't feel crowded, she was aware that he was close enough so he could touch her anytime he chose.

"I've been here about five years now."

"Really?"

"That surprises you?"

Elyssa took another sip from her wine glass, then set it down on the table. "I just thought it was—" she paused, searching for the appropriate response "—The decor seems newer than that."

"It's about five years old, too." He leaned forward slightly. "You don't like it?"

His bluntness caught her by surprise.

"I didn't say that," she denied quickly, shaking her head. "It's very well done." She glanced around, then looked back at him. "It even goes with your wardrobe," she concluded with a little smile, indicating the tailored black trousers and crisp white cotton shirt he had on.

Alex glanced down at himself as though just noticing what he was wearing. "Purely by chance, I assure you."

"I didn't *think* you were the kind of man who coordinated his clothes with his couch," she responded lightly.

"No?" There was a hint of challenge in his whiskey-colored eyes. "What kind of man do you think I am, then? Aside from—how did you put it that first night in the restaurant? Oh, yes. You said I didn't strike you as a man who did anything without a reason.''

Elyssa forced herself to sustain his gaze steadily. ''You still don't strike me that way.''

''And beyond that?''

She finally looked away. Off in the distance, there was a rumble of thunder. ''Beyond that, I haven't quite figured out.''

''But you're trying to.''

Blue eyes met brown-gold ones again. ''Yes.''

Alex took another swallow of wine. ''Is that why you came here tonight?''

Elyssa felt her cheeks flame and her heart skip a beat.

''I came here tonight because I wanted to, Alex,'' she answered after a few seconds. It was the truth, as far as it went. She'd *needed* to come here tonight. She'd needed to see him again. She couldn't explain the attraction that drew her to this man. She only knew that it existed and that it was virtually irresistible.

Alex scrutinized Elyssa for several long moments, noting the flush on her face and the frantic pulse of the vein at the base of her slim throat. He saw confusion in her delicately sculpted features and questions in her wide-set eyes, but there was no hint that she was hiding anything.

Could he forgive her if she'd truly forgotten him? he suddenly wondered.

Maybe.

Could he forgive her if she'd been another man's wife when they'd been together on Isla de la Corazón?

Probably not.

Could he forgive her if she'd had his daughter and kept her from him?

Never.

Alex stroked the stem of his wine glass. It was cool and hard against his fingertips. A poor substitute for the warm, soft skin of the woman sitting next to him.

Could he desire where he couldn't forgive?

Yes. God help him. Yes, he could.

''I'm glad you wanted to, Elyssa,'' he said finally. ''Very glad.'' He drained the remainder of the wine in his glass, then put it down on the table. After a moment, he plucked a plump cherry tomato off the platter and dipped it into one of the sauces. "Crudité?" he inquired.

Elyssa blinked. The abrupt change of subject would have been bewildering enough. But she'd been half-mesmerized by the seductive movement of Alex's strong fingers as well. There'd been a heady instant when she'd felt those fingers touching her...not the wine glass.

"Oh...oh, yes," she murmured finally. "Thank you."

She expected Alex to slide the platter closer to her at this point. Instead, he extended the succulent-looking tomato he'd selected, obviously intending to feed it to her.

For a split second, reality seemed to waver. Elyssa experienced the same disorienting sensation she'd felt when she'd first seen the orchids he'd sent. Everything around her blurred and shimmered as though an iridescent veil had been dropped over eyes.

She'd eaten food from a man's fingers before. She couldn't actually remember doing so, but every fiber of her being told her she'd done so and relished the experience.

Somewhere...

Sometime...

Elyssa tried to grasp the memory, but it was as insubstantial as a wisp of smoke. The feeling of déjà vu dissolved. Her vision cleared and reality snapped back into focus. Alex was still offering the tomato, his eyes fixed on her face.

Elyssa leaned forward slowly. She bit down on the tomato. It split open with a juicy spurt, the flavor of the pulp marrying deliciously with the tangy taste of the dipping sauce. She swallowed, then straightened. As she did so, Alex popped the remaining piece of the hors d'oeuvre into his own mouth. Whether he'd intended the gesture to be an erotic one didn't matter. It was. It bespoke a shared intimacy that made Elyssa's pulse scramble and her nervous system sing.

"Good?" He licked away a tomato seed caught in the right corner of his lips.

She nodded once, not trusting her voice.

"More?"

"Not—" her breath seemed to solidify at the top of her throat "—right now."

Alex eyed her curiously for a moment, then selected another cherry tomato, swirled it through the second dipping sauce, and ate it. "So," he said when he'd chewed and swallowed, "we were discussing your opinion of my apartment."

Elyssa fingered the skirt of her dress. She'd gone through her entire wardrobe three times before settling on it. "I told you," she answered. "I think it's very well done."

"But you don't like it."

"It's not a matter of liking or disliking. It's just—just—"

"Just what?"

Elyssa frowned, wondering why he was pursuing the matter so tenaciously. "I can't picture you living here, Alex," she finally told him.

"Mmm." His gaze shifted from her face to the sweeping expanse of glass and the vista it provided.

"Please." Elyssa impulsively reached out and laid her hand on his arm. She felt him tense at her touch and broke the contact. "Don't be offended."

He looked back at her, the gold flecks in his eyes glinting. "I'm not," he responded with a hint of ruefulness. "You aren't the first person to say something like that."

"Oh?" A decidedly unpleasant emotion uncoiled in the pit of Elyssa's stomach. It was an emotion she couldn't remember experiencing before.

"A friend once told me that what I do here falls under the category of occupying space."

Like a poisonous snake, the emotion hissed out the obvious possibility. The "friend" was a woman. A lover.

Elyssa picked up a piece of broccoli and ate it in three snapping bites. She disposed of a carrot stick with equal swiftness, then drank down the rest of her wine.

"That's very blunt," she observed. "Whoever said it must be a good friend."

"The best," Alex answered. "Philip is probably the only person in the world who'll tell me the truth whether I want to hear it or not."

Elyssa froze, her hand poised over the platter of crudités. She turned to look at Alex. "Philip?" she repeated.

She saw something she couldn't decipher flicker through the depths of Alex's eyes. She had the impression the reference to "Philip" had slipped out.

"Philip Lassiter," Alex elaborated after a second. "My lawyer."

"And . . . your best friend."

"Yes."

Neither of them spoke for several moments. Alex withdrew into himself, much as he'd done the previous weekend during lunch with Sandy. His angular features hardened, his lips thinned. But, as forbidding as his expression was, Elyssa felt impelled to breach the barrier it was obviously intended to be.

"Where *do* you live, Alex?" she asked softly.

He looked at her blankly. "What?"

"If you just occupy space here, where do you live— really?"

His introverted gaze turned outward again and he focused on her with spotlight intensity. He opened his mouth as though to reply to her question, then shut it again. For a few seconds, the only sound in the room was the splattering of countless raindrops against the windows.

"Alex?" Elyssa finally prompted, watching the subtle shift of muscle beneath the taut, tanned skin of his face. She could sense him wrestling with himself.

"I live where I work," he said briefly. "I . . . always have."

The hesitation in the last part of his response puzzled her. "And you always will?"

Again, Alex seemed to hesitate.

"I don't know," he answered eventually. "I have a place—" He broke off abruptly, cocking his head.

"What?" Elyssa questioned uncertainly. Concentrating, she thought she heard some kind of high-pitched buzz emanating from another part of the apartment. It was momentarily masked by a crackle of thunder.

Alex rose to his feet in a swift, seamless movement. "Dinner," he announced succinctly, then extended his right hand to her.

* * *

"That was absolutely delicious," Elyssa declared about two hours later. She sighed contentedly and settled back against the leather sofa.

"You liked the paella?" Alex inquired, sitting down beside her and stretching his long, black-clad legs out in front of him. He was cradling a snifter of brandy in his right hand.

Elyssa turned her head in a lazy movement, vaguely registering that several of the pins she'd used to secure her hair popped loose as she did so. "Actually, no," she confided, savoring the memory of saffron-spiced rice and succulent seafood. "I only ate three servings to be polite."

Alex chuckled. "I see." He swirled the brandy around in the snifter, then took a sip.

"For someone who claims he only cooks occasionally, you're very good at it."

"Thank you."

Elyssa let her eyes drift slowly over the man next to her, thinking about the deftness he'd demonstrated in the kitchen. His skill had surprised her at first. Then she'd realized it was in keeping with everything she knew about his nature. She had the distinct impression that anything Alexander Moran took the time to do, he took the time to do extremely well. What she wasn't certain of was whether this was due to a keen competitive instinct, an intolerance of incompetence, or both.

Her gaze settled on Alex's hands for a moment. He was cupping the snifter in both palms now, his long, lean fingers curving to match its rounded shape. While he obviously possessed the strength to shatter the fragile glass, he also gave the impression that he could have held a soap bubble without bursting it.

Elyssa swallowed and shifted her eyes upward a little. Alex had rolled back his sleeves earlier, revealing sun-darkened forearms. They were whorled with the same brown hair that dusted the back of his hands and marked the wedge-shaped piece of chest left bare by his open-collared white shirt. The hair looked soft and silky, in stark contrast to the ridges of muscle and tendon it partially covered.

She swallowed again, conscious that there were tendrils of heat curling and uncurling deep within her stomach. The rhythm of her pulse altered. So did her breathing pattern. Her gaze slowly slid upward . . . upward . . .

"See anything you like?"

The inquiry insinuated itself so smoothly into Elyssa's mind that it took her a moment or two to identify its source. The embarrassing realization of how blatantly she'd been assessing Alex followed a split second later.

"N-no," she stammered. She darted what she intended to be a quick glance at Alex's face. The intention was obliterated by the connection that formed the instant her eyes met his.

"No?"

"Yes," she contradicted herself. Her thoughts were stampeding in a dozen different directions. She tried to corral and control at least one of them. "I mean, I don't . . ." She made a vague gesture, then concluded lamely, "I'm . . . I'm sorry I was staring at you."

"Don't be," Alex returned softly. "It gave me a chance to stare at you."

Elyssa didn't know what to say to this. She lifted one hand and patted at her hair with unsteady fingers.

Alex took a slow sip of brandy, still holding her gaze over the rim of the glass. "Aren't you going to ask whether I saw anything I liked?" he inquired, cocking a brow.

Elyssa opened her mouth to say something. Exactly what, she could never recall. The words were forestalled by a brilliant flare of lightning and a deep rumble of thunder. She shivered, her toes curling inside her shoes. The tips of her fingers tingled.

She lifted her chin a notch. "Did you?" she countered in a voice that wasn't quite her own.

Elyssa saw Alex's dark eyes spark gold, then narrow suspiciously. She watched his entire manner go from at ease to alert in the space of a second. It was obvious that her provocative question had surprised him.

It had surprised her, too. Flirtation was an art she'd never mastered, despite the years she'd spent desperately trying to be the "good" girl who pleased everyone. The games men and women played had always been a mystery to her. Her former financé had been scathingly specific about her lack of aptitude in that area.

Alex set down the brandy snifter with almost ritualistic precision, then shifted his body closer to Elyssa's. His left leg pressed briefly against her right one, mating them from ankle to thigh for a moment.

"Yes," he replied very quietly. There was another rumble of thunder. "Everything I saw, I liked."

His hands came up to cup her face. Gently. Very gently. He caressed her temples and cheeks with his fingers and used his thumbs to stroke coaxingly beneath her chin. His touch was devastatingly sensual. It was also as delicate as the feathering of a hummingbird's wing.

Elyssa's lips parted. The air in her lungs came out in a shaky rush. "Alex," she whispered, raising her own hands to trace the hard planes and striking hollows of his face. She could feel the unyielding bone beneath the tanned skin. A hint of new beard growth sandpapered her fingertips.

The first time he'd kissed her had been fast and fierce. No preliminaries, just an explosion of heat and hunger. This time, the buildup was much more controlled. The passage of seconds was like the flow of honey—slow and sweet. Whether Alex was teasing her or testing himself, Elyssa didn't know.

She was trembling with eagerness when he finally bent his dark head and kissed her. She yielded everything he asked for and more. She willingly let him taste his fill of the soft depths behind her lips. She licked at the corners of his mouth with the tip of her tongue, savoring the groan of response this drew from him.

Alex's arms came around her. His palms caressed her. Captured her. Elyssa slid her own hands down from his face to his broad shoulders, her fingers pressing into the taut muscles beneath his white cotton shirt. His embrace tightened, drawing her closer.

"Sweet," he murmured huskily. "So sweet." He caught her lower lip between his teeth, nipping at the tender flesh with exquisitely calibrated care. A ragged whimper escaped her throat.

"Alex. Oh . . . Alex."

Slowly, seductively, he began easing her back against the sofa. Her bones turned to water. The blood in her veins fizzed like uncorked champagne.

And then:

A flash of lightning.

A crash of thunder.

The sudden jangle of a phone in a nearby room.

Whether Alex stiffened because she did or vice versa, Elyssa never knew. It didn't really matter. The fabric of heedless passion began to unravel.

Her eyelids fluttered open. There was another bright burst of lightning, another boom of thunder. She flinched against the sight and sound. Her heart was hammering so hard she was afraid it might crack her ribs from the inside.

The phone kept ringing.

Alex's eyes were open, too. For an instant, he looked shattered and unsure. Then comprehension seemed to re-shape his features into a mask of endurance. A deep flush stained the angled ledge of his cheekbones.

"Oh, God," he groaned harshly. He sounded like a man in agony.

Elyssa understood his pain. Her entire body burned. "A-Alex . . . what?"

The phone continued to shrill its imperious summons.

"Business line in the study," he explained thickly. "Forgot . . . the machine."

His words didn't make much sense to Elyssa, but the shifting of his weight and the easing of his embrace communicated his intention very clearly.

And still, the phone went on ringing.

"No!" It was plea and protest together. Elyssa reached out to him as he rose to his feet. The idea that Alex would leave her now was unbearable. She knew he had a good reason for going, but what if he didn't return?

What if . . . what if . . .

The sense of past and present coming together enveloped her like a cloud, blurring the distinctions between then and now, between the vaguely remembered and very real.

A man had left her.

Somewhere...
Sometime...
She'd never seen him again.
"Alex—"
"I'll be back," he promised and turned on his heel.
"I'll be waiting," she whispered.

Alex slammed the telephone receiver back into is cradle and punched the switch that turned on his answering machine. He'd just had word of a new deal ready to be signed, sealed, and delivered.

He didn't give a damn. He didn't give a damn about anything except the woman in the next room.

I'll be waiting, she'd told him.

She'd made the pledge so softly. So, so softly. But he'd heard her nonetheless. And hearing her repeat that simple three-word promise after so many years had nearly killed him.

Alex balled his hands into fists as a shudder that was half anger, half anguish, shook him.

The feel of her body moving in arousing conterpoint to his. The faint, floral scent of her soft skin. The sweet taste and sleek texture of her mouth. The throaty sound of her voice saying his name.

Memories of her—of how it had been between them just minutes before—flooded his senses. Alex fought against the rising tide of erotic recollections.

He hadn't invited Elyssa here tonight to seduce her. To question her, yes. He'd intended to inquire. To observe her reactions. To absorb her responses. That was all!

Alex inhaled sharply. He felt like a blind man trying to put together a puzzle. Each time it seemed he might be on the verge of putting the picture together, he discovered a piece he hadn't known existed or realized a piece he'd thought he possessed wasn't there.

He released his breath slowly. His "intentions" for this evening didn't matter anymore. He couldn't wait any longer. He had to confront her. Here. Now. It was time to face the truth, whatever that truth might be.

* * *

She was standing by the windows, staring out at the storm, when he returned to her. She'd unpinned her hair and she was languidly combing the cornsilk strands with the fingers of her left hand. The unconscious sensuality of the gesture affected Alex like a caress. He felt his body stir and stiffen.

He moved toward her slowly, silently. Finally, he was close enough to stretch out his hand and touch her.

She turned.

He forgot how to breathe.

Her eyes were huge and dreamy, the pupils dilated until only a narrow ring of sapphire showed around the edges of her irises. There was a blush of pink in her cheeks, the same pink that had tinted the frilled petals of the orchids he'd sent her. Her lips were slightly parted, as though she intended to speak.

A grating sound clawed its way up out of his throat.

She didn't say a word. She simply offered him a smile.

Alex knew the smile. The curving beauty of it had been captured in a snapshot he'd carried with him for more than six and a half years.

He said the name of the woman in that snapshot.

A moment later, she was in his arms.

Five

<hr/>

Alexander Moran was only human.

For years he had dreamed of this. Ached for it. Lived on the mind-searing memory of what it was like to hold this woman in this way. He would have found it infinitely easier to turn his back on everything he'd achieved in his thirty-six years than to refuse what he was being offered at this moment.

"Dawn," he groaned from the very depth of his soul.

"Yes," she breathed, and melted against him.

She tipped her head back, her throat curving like the stem of a flower, her blond hair rippling away from her face. Her cheeks were flushed, her nostrils delicately flared. Her soft, ripe mouth was a temptation Alex could not resist.

He brought his head down. Their lips met in a deep, devouring kiss. If he had wanted proof of heaven, it came in that first blissful instant of contact and claiming.

Dawn opened to him. He possessed the sweetness of her mouth with one bold stroke of his tongue. Tasting. Tantalizing. Triggering a response that was so honest it threatened to undo him then and there.

Slim fingers framed his face for a moment before sliding back, spreading wide and tangling deep in his hair. Dawn's tongue partnered his in a sinuous, sensuous dance. She nipped at his lower lip, catching it between the slightly serrated edge of her front teeth, then caressing it with a slow, catlike lick. Alex shuddered. The masculine weight between his legs increased tenfold in a single, sizzling second.

He tightened his embrace, holding her close. She arched against him, fitting her soft body to his much harder one. Every promising, provocative movement she made was a potent reminder of how perfectly they had complemented each other during the time they'd had together in a passionate paradise called Corazón.

Desire consumed him the way a flame consumes a fuse.

Alex said her name. The sound of his voice was rough and raw. He stroked one hand down her back, mapping the line of her spine, molding the firm, feminine roundness of her bottom. He kneaded her through the fabric of her dress and whatever she wore beneath it, then rocked her against the taut cradle of his thighs.

He brought his other hand up to cup the back of her skull. He wove his fingers through her hair, controlling the movement of her head, angling her face so he could claim an even more intimate access to her mouth. He feasted on the hot, honeyed taste of her, exploring the moist mysteries behind her lips with delving strokes of his tongue.

Dawn's hands slipped downward from his hair. She scored the back of Alex's neck lightly with her nails and assessed the arrogant strength of his shoulders with her palms. She made a murmurous sound that was as approving as it was arousing.

And then she discovered the triangle of flesh revealed by the open collar of his shirt. She defined the area with slow-moving fingertips, stirring the fine brown hair and savoring the supple skin beneath.

"Yes," Alex growled harshly, gritting his teeth against her sweetly tormenting touch. Need twisted like a knife blade in his loins. "Oh, God. Yes."

He eased away from her just enough to slide a hand between their bodies. He sought and found the tightly wrapped belt that held her dress together. After a few frustrating moments, the knot in the belt began to come loose.

A twist of his wrist.

A tug of his fingers.

Dawn's dress opened from throat to knee. A moment later, the garment was in a heathery rose heap on the floor, leaving her clad in little more than a pale pink slip, panty hose, and pearls.

Alex sucked in his breath as he studied her with passionate, possessive intensity. The slip clung snugly to the curves of her breasts. They looked fuller than he remembered, and the shadowed cleft between them seemed deeper. The taut shape of her budding nipples was clearly visible through the champagne lace insets of the slip's bodice. He vividly recalled what it was like to take those plush velvet peaks deep into his mouth.

"Beautiful," he whispered, his breath catching in his throat. "So very beautiful."

"For you," she whispered back. "Only for you."

Dawn swayed a little then, like a blossom in a breeze. He caught her to him, taking her mouth in another slow, searching kiss. As her lips parted to accept the evocative thrust of his tongue, he swept her up into his arms and carried her off to his bedroom.

Desire hammered at him every step of the way, almost bringing him to his knees once or twice. The force of what he felt for her was staggering, but he somehow found the strength to stay on his feet.

Like the area they had just left, his bedroom was a spartan study in neutral shades. It, too, had a wall that was dominated by a bold sweep of windows.

Alex laid Dawn down on his bed gently, but did not immediately stretch out beside her. She reached for him, her fingertips grazing his forearm. Her passion-rouged mouth shaped his name like a prayer. She did not seem to have the breath to actually say it aloud.

She had lost her left shoe somewhere along the line. Alex bent and slipped off her right one, dropping it carelessly on the floor beside the bed. He cupped her stockinged feet in his hands, rubbing his hard palms along her soles until her pink-polished toes pointed like a dancer's. Then, slowly, he began to stroke upward.

From ankle to calf. He paused, massaging the subtle swell of muscle that helped define the graceful lines of her lower legs.

From calf to knee. He stopped there, too, fingers finessing the softly creased flesh, finding the spot where her blood pulsed just beneath the skin.

From knee to thigh. He felt a tremor of anticipation become an unmistakable shudder of arousal as he moved his palms slowly, oh so slowly, over the creamy, nylon-clad flesh.

Alex shifted his gaze for a moment. Dawn had levered herself up on her elbows. Her head was tilted back a little, and she was watching him caress her from beneath heavy, half-closed lids. The dreamily intent expression on her fair-skinned face made him burn to the marrow of his bones.

Their eyes met. Alex saw her lips part to reveal the edges of her teeth and the curling tip of her pink tongue. He watched her breasts rise on a sudden intake of breath. The twin peaks of her nipples strained against the slip's lacy top.

The impulse to take her then and there was very, very strong. It would have been so easy to strip off the clothes that separated them and sheath himself deep within her. There was no doubt Dawn was willing. It was clear the emotions driving him were driving her as well. They were both intent on arriving at the same ecstatic destination...together.

Yet Alex resisted the clamor for consummation. There was no hesitation in this holding back. It was not prompted by any doubts about what they were doing. He had never been more certain about the rightness of something in his entire life.

Perhaps it was a touch of perversity that made him decide to wait. Perversity, and a powerful desire to prolong the pleasure for both of them. He had always thought he would rush to reclaim Dawn in the fastest, most fiercely elemental fashion possible if fate ever granted him the opportunity to do so. But now that it had, he found no need to hurry. This woman was utterly, absolutely his. And he was utterly, absolutely hers. He knew they belonged to each other in a way that went far beyond any act of physical joining.

Alex slid his hand under her slip and up to Dawn's waist. Hooking his fingers beneath the elastic at the top of her panty hose, he began to tug. She lifted her hips an inch or two, her head tilting back even further than before.

He peeled the sheer nylon stockings down her legs and cast them aside. A second after that, he kicked off his shoes and joined her on the bed.

"Dawn. Sweet Dawn..."

"Alex. Oh, Alex..."

She came into his arms again, her mouth an offering, the movements of her body an invitation. He accepted both without hesitation. The fingers of his right hand combed back through her hair then fisted, capturing countless hundreds of silken strands in a possessive grasp. The fingers of his left hand skimmed down to caress her right breast through the fragile lace of her slip. He rubbed the pad of his thumb across her nipple and heard her whimper deep in her throat. The sound was as intoxicating as wine.

After a few moments, Alex became aware of Dawn's hands moving against his chest, plucking at the buttons on the front of his shirt. The garment parted suddenly. She pulled it free of the fitted waistband of his trousers with an impatient tug, then pressed her palms against his naked chest. Fanning her fingers wide, she began winnowing through the coarse silk hair that whorled across his skin.

Inevitably she found the knotted buttons of his nipples. He groaned in something very close to agony as she flicked the violently sensitive bits of flesh with the edges of her nails. The white-hot sensation she triggered darted through his nervous system like an electrical current arrows along a copper wire.

Dawn nibbled at his mouth, then nuzzled a path to his ear. After licking at the lobe as though it were some exotic treat, she kissed a trail down the side of his neck. She teased him with her teeth and tongue. Even her breath, bathing his skin like a warm mist, seemed designed to ravish his senses.

"Please," she whispered. "Please, I want..."

"I want, too, love," he assured her thickly.

He stroked one hand down her body until he reached the lace-trimmed hem of her slip. It had already ridden up to the top of her thighs. He pulled it still higher, baring her to the waist.

Dawn quivered when he brushed his fingertips against the silken triangle of hair that sheltered her most intimate secrets. The cluster of curls was as soft as he remembered. So was the layered femininity beneath.

She had wept with a kind of stunned joy the first time he'd caressed her there, wordlessly telling him how little she understood about the gift of her own sensuality. He heard her sob now as he gently parted the petalled flesh to find the tiny nub which held the key to a pleasure so intense he knew it was almost pain.

He touched her. Once. Twice. Three times.

His fingertips grew slick with the dew of her response.

"Oh...oh...oh..." Dawn's voice rose with each syllable, finally splintering on a peak of sensation.

An unknowable time later, Alex rolled away and stood up. He shucked off his shirt and tossed it aside. His trousers and briefs followed a few seconds later. He was harder than he had ever been in his life.

He saw—virtually felt—Dawn's gaze move over him. Her eyes widened just a little when they settled on the rigid evidence of his arousal. He experienced a heart-stopping instant of anxiety.

A sudden flash of lightning bathed the room in an unearthly silver glow. A moment later it faded and there was a rumble of thunder.

Dawn extended one hand toward him in a slow, graceful gesture. She drew the other up along her body, her pink-nailed fingers drifting over her naked belly and through the valley that divided her breasts. They finally came to rest against the strand of pearls that still circled her throat.

"Yes," she said huskily, answering the question he hadn't voiced.

Alex went to her.

There had been a hint of shyness about Dawn on Corazón. A touch of uncertainty. For this reason, Alex had been

tenderly cautious when they'd loved. He'd wanted no taint
of shock or shame to spoil what they had together.

Now, however, he sensed no shyness, sensed no uncertainty. While tenderness was still key to his erotic intentions, the need for caution seemed to have been swept away
by the passage of time.

Alex kissed his way down her body by slow, searing
stages. He stopped to suckle at her breasts, drawing her
nipples into quivering crowns and leaving the fabric that
covered them damp and clinging. The shallow dimple of her
navel riveted his attention next. He circled the shadowed
indentation with his tongue and saw the muscles just beneath the skin of her stomach flutter.

Ultimately his mouth claimed the warm, womanly softness he'd explored with his fingers only a few moments before.

Dawn gave a wild, choked cry. Her body shivered in convulsive response to his loving caress. She clutched at his dark
hair.

He bathed her with lapping strokes of his tongue. Nibbled her teasingly with his teeth. The touch of his lips was
the very essence of intimacy. He coaxed her to the edge of
ecstasy, then urged her over. He heard her sob, felt her
shudder. Her pleasure was his pleasure and he was greedy
for both of them.

Finally, knowing that his ability to control himself was
almost gone, Alex moved up and over the woman he had
yearned for, dreamed about, and prayed to find again for
more than six and a half years. He slid his hands beneath her
hips, palms cupping her bottom for an instant, then gliding
down to the back of her legs. His fingers moved against the
tender inner flesh of her upper thighs. She yielded eagerly,
parting her legs farther and farther apart.

"Y-yes...yes. Please..." Dawn moaned, her head moving
back and forth in the tangle of her perspiration-darkened
hair. "Alex..."

He felt her shift suddenly as the hard length of his male-
ness brushed against the cleft of her womanhood. The
movements made his entire body clench and go rigid.

Alex could wait no longer. The steel cables of self-discipline with which he had controlled his life for so many years had snapped. Restraint was reduced to a fragile, fraying thread.

He joined them in a single plunging thrust. Dawn arched up, taking him deeper into herself than he had ever dreamed of going.

She was all sweet, yielding heat. Her body accepted his fully, then tightened to the point of torment. He looked down into her face. Blue eyes locked with brown-gold ones.

"So... beautiful..." Alex groaned raggedly.

"So...strong...so...ohhh..." Her words unraveled on a gasping sigh.

Which one of them began moving first, Alex couldn't say. He didn't care. It didn't matter. Everything that was happening to them, between them, was shared and he knew that never, *never,* in his life had he been so close to another person.

"Dawn..."

"Al...ex..."

Her arms went up, locking around his neck, bringing his face down to hers. Their lips met, their tongue mated, the fragments of their breath married.

He felt the first rippling contraction of completion sweep through Dawn as though he, himself, was experiencing it. A second later, he found his own pulsing release. It spilled out of him with explosive force. He could no more have held it back than he could have stopped the storm that still buffeted the city outside.

She cried out his name, her passion-shattered voice turning the few brief syllables into broken but beautiful music.

"Dawn...love..." he rasped in reply.

Alexander Moran was only human. So, he knew, was the woman moving beneath him. Yet what they created together in the endless, ecstatic time that followed seemed to him to have been divinely ordained.

Afterward, Dawn fell asleep in Alex's arms. She curled up against him, her cheek resting on the spot over his heart.

Her breath eddied across his chest like the gentlest of spring breezes. If he shifted, she moved with him.

Sleep beckoned, but Alex tried to stay awake. He wanted to savor the dream that had come true after more than six and a half aching, empty years. He wanted to steep himself in the knowledge that Dawn was really there and really his once again.

Her face was partially hidden by her hair. He brushed the pale gold strands back with tender fingers, teasing the outer curve of her ear as he did so. She murmured something he couldn't make out. The smile that reshaped her lips was infinitely easier to comprehend.

"Dawn," he whispered softly, settling her even more intimately against him. Her sleek legs tangled briefly with his hair-roughened ones. She twisted a little and the tips of her breasts brushed his upper arm.

Alex took a deep breath, inhaling the scent of her skin. The elusive floral fragrance of her perfume was now mixed with the musk of sensual satiation.

He had, as he has told Philip, lived with the possibilities that this woman might be dead or that her disappearance from Isla de la Corazón might have been a deliberate act of desertion. He had not allowed himself to admit until now how deeply ingrained his acceptance of those possibilities had become. He had never lost hope completely, but he had come very close.

There was a distant rumble of thunder. Alex felt Dawn tense and then begin to tremble. She whimpered wordlessly and shook her head.

"Shhh. I'm here," he assured her quickly, keeping his voice low. He stroked her soothingly, moving his hand slowly up her body from knee to breast. He continued to caress her until she stopped trembling and relaxed against him once more. She sighed softly, her warm breath fanning across his chest.

"Yes, sweetheart," Alex whispered huskily. "Everything's all right."

But was it?

He closed his eyes for a moment, his hand stilling, his heart skipping a beat.

No, he corrected. Everything *wasn't* all right. There were still questions to be answered, truths to be faced. Until that happened, very little would be all right. And even once it did...

Alex opened his eyes and stared up at the ceiling, recalling the soul-searching catechism he had put to himself what now seemed a long, long time ago.

Could he forgive her if she'd truly forgotten him?

Could he forgive her if she'd been another man's wife when they'd been together on Isla de la Corazón?

Could he forgive her if she'd had his daughter and kept her from him?

Could he desire where he couldn't forgive?

Could he love?

A little over seven days before, he'd stood on the terrace of his apartment and silently admitted that what he felt for Elyssa Dawn Collins was love. It had taken him years to put a name to the emotion. He'd tried many others. Want. Need. Hunger. Obsession. But, in the end, he had arrived at—or had he come back to?—love.

Yet he'd admitted to loving before he knew about Sandy. *Sandy.* The brown-eyed, brown-haired little pixie who could be his daughter. His only child. If she was, and if the woman now sleeping beside him had kept her a secret from him...

God! Could a man hate where he also loved?

Elyssa stirred. Alex tightened his embrace. At the same time, he turned his head away from her and looked toward the windows. He listened to the splash of raindrops against the glass for several long moments.

There had to be an explanation he hadn't thought of. A possibility he hadn't considered. He simply could not bring himself to believe that the gentle, generous woman he held in his arms was capable of the kind of cruelty involved in deliberately deceiving a husband, a lover, and an innocent child.

Tomorrow, he promised himself, fighting to suppress a sudden yawn. Tomorrow I'll have the truth.

Elyssa murmured once again. This time Alex was certain what she was saying was his name.

Tomorrow...

I'll be waiting.

It was his last coherent thought before sleep overcame him.

The sun was shining brightly when Alex awoke hours later.

The storm of the night before was over.

Elyssa Dawn Collins was gone.

Six

What had she done?

Elyssa sat on the edge of the chintz-covered couch in her living room, hugging herself with her arms, trying to come to grips with the enormity of what had happened the night before. She shivered. A moan of distress welled up from deep within her.

God. Oh, God.

She rocked forward and back. Forward and back.

Elyssa didn't know how much time had passed since she'd fled Alexander Moran's apartment to seek refuge in her own home. More than minutes. Less than days. She was too confused, too conflicted, to have any better sense of it than that.

She would never forget the shock of waking up to find herself in Alex's arms. *Never.* Heaven knew that she would if she could, but she couldn't.

There had been a few moments when the line between slumber and consciousness had been blurred. A few moments when she'd been wrapped in the most rapturous kind of contentment she'd ever known. No shame. No uncertainty. Just an intoxicating sense of being where she belonged.

The feel of a hard male body pressing against her more pliant feminine one.

The cup of a possessive palm around one of her breasts.

The tantalizing fan of someone's breath over her cheek.

The slow and steady beat of someone's heart beneath her ear.

She'd thought she must be dreaming. And then she'd realized she wasn't.

She'd realized she hadn't been dreaming before, either.

The sensuous search of a mouth against hers.

The questing caress of long, lean fingers over her skin.

The hoarse and husky sound of a deep voice repeating her name.

The unbearably beautiful sensation of being filled so carefully, so completely, it made her want to weep with pleasure.

It had been real. All of it had been real!

Echoes of ecstasy reverberated in Elyssa's brain. A shimmering wave of heat washed through her body. She felt a throb of longing between her thighs. Her nipples stiffened against the nubby fabric of the shapeless terry cloth bathrobe in which she'd wrapped herself sometime earlier.

The rumpled garments she'd been wearing when she'd returned to her Greenwich Village apartment now lay discarded on the tiled floor of the bathroom. She'd stripped them off as though they'd been contaminated. The heathery rose wrap dress. The pale pink, lace-trimmed slip. The sheer nude-toned panty hose. She didn't know how long it would be before she would be able to bring herself to touch those things—much less wear them—again.

She'd located the slip amid the musk-scented sheets of Alex's bed. He'd stirred and said something on a questioning inflection as she'd started to pull it out of the tangled linen. She'd frozen, terrified he might wake up. Finally he'd rolled over, buried his face in the pillow where her head had lain only a minute or two before, and gone still.

Nerves jangling, pulse jittering, she'd then bent to recover her panty hose and one of her shoes from the bedroom's carpeted floor. She'd tiptoed out, scarcely daring to breathe, then stumbled over the second shoe in the hall that led to the living room.

It was in the living room that she'd reclaimed her dress. The recollection of how willingly she'd let it be stripped from her body had scalded her brain as she'd put it back on.

She had no idea what had happened to the strand of pearls she'd been wearing. No idea at all.

Elyssa bit the inside of her cheek, almost welcoming the self-inflicted pain. A second later, she tasted the copper-salt tang of her blood. She choked back a sob. The memories she wanted to keep at bay rushed in on her.

The storm.

Thunder. Lightning.

Driving, drenching rains. Howling, hungry winds. Silver-capped waves smashing against a white sand shore.

The dream.

Kisses. Caresses.

Sweet heaven, she'd never known it could be like this! She'd never known she could need and be needed so utterly, so absolutely. She'd never known that she could give with such wild and wonderful freedom, that she could receive with such fierce and feverish greed. Yes. Oh... yes, please. Yes!

Past and present, coming together. Binding. Last night. Other nights. The overwhelming sense that what had happened had happened before.

Somewhere...

Sometime...

Thunder. Lightning.

Kisses. Caresses.

The lover.

Alexander Moran.

"No," Elyssa whispered starkly, shaking her head.

The stranger.

Alexander Moran.

"No," she repeated, clenching her hands until her knuckles turned white and her nails dug deep into the flesh of her palms.

Alexander Moran.

The father of her—

"*No!*" she cried out, trying to sunder the last link in the inexorably forming chain of logic. "No! It isn't possible!"

Elyssa pressed trembling fingers to tender lips. She knew her mouth was slightly swollen. She'd seen how ripe it looked when she'd caught a glimpse of herself in the mirror over the bathroom sink. She'd also seen the rosy abrasion at the base of her throat and the faint smudge of a bruise on the upper curve of her right breast.

Alexander Moran had left his mark on her...in more ways than one.

Elyssa drew a shuddery breath, drawing the air into her lungs in ratcheting little gulps.

It couldn't be, she told herself. It just couldn't be!

Alex Moran, the faceless, nameless stranger who haunted her in her storm-inspired dreams?

Alex Moran, the temporary lover she'd surrendered to— or been seduced by—on Isla de la Corazón?

Alex Moran, the man who'd fathered Sandy?

No!

Elyssa sprang up, every fiber of her being quivering in resistance to the thoughts exploding within her head. She was under bombardment from an enemy out of her past and she had pitifully few weapons with which she could defend herself.

"He didn't know me," she said aloud, arguing with herself and whatever cruel-minded fates were bent on manipulating her. "If he...if Alex was the man on Corazón, he would have known me. He would have said something!"

Wouldn't he?

Unless...unless...

Elyssa began pacing back and forth in the cozy, cluttered confines of her blue-and-white living room.

Oh, God. Supposing Alexander Moran *had* been the man on Corazón. But supposing he'd been waiting for *her* to say something about their past relationship?

No. No. That didn't make sense! Why would he wait? Why would he keep silent? The man she knew would not—

Elyssa halted, a bitter laugh splintering in her throat.

The man she knew? She knew nothing!

She resumed her pacing.

There was another possibility, of course. And a very ugly possibility it was, too.

Perhaps Alex had been her lover on Corazón but had no desire to acknowledge the fact. Perhaps the earth-shattering ecstasy of her dreams was all a fantasy. Perhaps what had passed between them had been exactly what she'd always feared she might recall it as being: a meaningless one-night stand that had left her pregnant and him indifferent.

This possibility struck Elyssa as slightly more plausible—though hardly less painful—than the others for two reasons. The first was that she'd had exactly one lover before she'd come to Corazón, and she'd seen proof with her own eyes of her inability to please him. It seemed highly unlikely that she'd suddenly blossomed into a sensuous woman capable of inspiring the passions of a virtual stranger.

The second and even more compelling reason was the simple fact that her island lover, whomever he had been, had never tried to contact her. She'd been taken off Corazón injured and unconscious. If she'd mattered at all to the man she'd been with, wouldn't he have wanted to know what had happened to her?

What was it Alex had said that night over dinner when she'd asked him whether he'd ever searched for his father?

Oh, yes.

Why look for someone you don't want to find?

Callous, perhaps. But also very, very clear.

And yet . . .

Alex had called her Dawn. The lover in her dreams called her that, too.

He'd known about the freckles on her nose. And, for reasons she couldn't explain, that knowledge had struck a very intimate chord within her.

He'd sent her orchids that had tantalized her with intimations of another place and another time.

He'd also formed an undeniable bond with Sandy.

Elyssa shook her head violently, flinching from the thought of Alex and her daughter.

But what if he were—?

And what if he wanted—?

No. Sandy was her daughter. *Hers!*

Elyssa crossed back to the sofa and sank down against its plump cushions.

What if.

Perhaps.

Supposing.

Elyssa wrapped her arms around herself again. She knew she was going to have to confront the possibilities. She knew she was going to have to find out the truth, once and for all.

She had to stop running away from who she was...and what she'd done.

All right. What if, perhaps, supposing, Alexander Moran had nothing to do with whatever it was that had happened to her more than six and a half years ago on an island called Corazón?

What if, perhaps, supposing, he was simply a man she had wanted from the instant their eyes had met and their hands had touched less than three weeks before?

And what if, perhaps, supposing, he was a man with whom she seemed to become a person she didn't know? A person she wasn't at all certain she wanted to be?

I saw the way you looked when you came home last night, Lys, her friend Nikki had told her the day after Alex had kissed her for the first time.

How did I look? she'd asked, already knowing the answer.

You looked ravished, Nikki had replied. *Or maybe I mean ravishing. Maybe both. Ravished and ravishing. Oh, I don't know. You just didn't look like you, Lys! And it was obviously because of him. Alexander Moran. It—well, frankly, it scared me a little.*

It scared me a little, too, she'd responded after a few moments.

Elyssa realized she was trembling. She tried to stop, but she couldn't.

In the end, she was reduced to repeating the question she'd first whispered when she'd realized that she was lying naked in the arms of a lover who was flesh-and-blood reality, not a storm-induced fantasy.

"What have I done?"

Alex glared at the digital indicator that chronicled the measured descent of the elevator car in which he was riding.

17 . . . 16 . . . 15 . . .

Faster, dammit. Faster!

He stabbed viciously at the button marked Lobby with his index finger. Again and again and again, he hit it.

12 . . . 11 . . . 10 . . .

He'd woken perhaps ten minutes before to the discovery that the fragrant softness he was holding in his arms was a pillow that carried the hauntingly sweet smell of Elyssa's skin. Smiling a little, he'd rolled over, intending to call her name. Instead he'd grunted in surprise as a small but sharply pointed object jabbed him in the back. He'd shifted, fumbled beneath himself in the sheets for a second, then fished out a strand of pearls.

His memory had instantly flashed up the image of Elyssa touching those pearls with the fingertips of one hand while she extended the other toward him. His body had begun to stir and stiffen in response.

And then he'd realized.

He was alone.

Not simply alone in his bed. Alone in the apartment. He was too intimately acquainted with the echoing emptiness of solitude to be mistaken about the situation.

Elyssa was gone.

She'd left him.

Alex had called her name anyway.

There'd been no answer.

He'd kicked aside the sheets and gotten out of bed, one corner of his mind registering that the pair of panty hose and high-heeled pump he'd dropped on the floor the night before were no longer there. His own clothing—white shirt, black trousers, and shoes—remained where he'd tossed them.

It had been then that he'd started to curse.

Naked, he'd stalked through the entire apartment, conducting a search he knew was futile. The only traces of Elyssa's presence he had found were a few hairpins scattered on the carpet by the sliding terrace door in the living room.

He'd returned to his bedroom, still swearing with cold, killing precision. He'd stared for a few furious seconds at the evocative disorder of the bed, wondering whether the sheets held the warmth of Elyssa's body as well as her scent.

When he'd damned her a moment later, he'd meant it.

He'd dressed in the same clothes he'd worn the night before. Then, after pausing just long enough to snatch up his wallet and keys, he'd stormed out of his apartment. He'd vowed to have the truth from Elyssa this morning and have it he would! Wherever she'd run to, he'd find her. And once he did...

Ding!

The elevator came to a halt. Alex clenched and unclenched his hands.

Open, dammit. Open!

The doors slid apart.

Alex charged out of the elevator car like a bull. He took two steps and slammed into a fair-haired, medium-sized man in a beige trench coat. The man staggered, his arms windmilling as he tried to maintain his balance.

Afterward Alex thought he might have said he was sorry. He thought he might have checked his stride, too, when he realized the man he'd run into was Philip Lassiter. But he didn't stop. He definitely didn't stop. He didn't intend to stop for anyone or anything. He was going to find Elyssa and finally get the truth. That's all that mattered to him.

It didn't matter that Philip was calling his name.

It didn't matter that Philip was chasing after him.

It didn't matter that Philip was grabbing his arm.

It didn't matter that Philip was telling him—

Alex stopped. So, it seemed for a moment, did his heart.

He turned. Slowly. Very slowly. He moved like a man who'd suddenly found himself on the crumbling edge of a precipice. One wrong step and he'd tumble to his destruction.

"What did you say?" he demanded.

Philip squared his shoulders and took a deep breath. "I said, the agency couriered its preliminary findings on Elyssa Dawn Collins over to me this morning. She isn't a widow, Alex. She's never been married."

"*Never been married?* Alex repeated rawly. "You're telling me she lied about—"

"She was engaged to a man named Lane Edwards about seven years ago," Philip interrupted. He could have been reciting from a page in a phone book for all the emotion in his voice. "He was an executive with her stepfather's manufacturing company outside Chicago. She broke it off. Three weeks after she gave Edwards back his ring, she flew to Isla de la Corazón. Alone. Ten days later, the island—plus most of the rest of the Caribbean and a big piece of the U.S. Gulf coast—was devastated by one of the worst hurricanes of the century. Two days after that, she was flown into Galveston on a med-evac helicopter. She had some kind of head injury and she was unconscious."

Alex's stomach knotted. His throat closed up. As angry as he was at Elyssa for leaving him, the thought of her having been hurt was almost more than he could bear.

"She remained unconscious—and unidentified—for nearly forty-eight hours," Philip went on levelly. "When she came to, she was able to tell doctors who she was. But she had no idea what had happened to her. She had no memory of ever having been on Isla de la Corazón."

Alex stared at his friend, too stunned by this revelation to speak. No memory? he thought, trying to process the concept through a brain that seemed to have gone into some kind of overload condition. Was Philip saying—?

"The diagnosis was amnesia caused by a blow to the head," the other man reported, answering the question Alex couldn't voice. "A week later, she was discharged and went home to her mother and stepfather. Less than two months after that, she moved to New York."

Alex swallowed convulsively. He ran his hand back through his hair. His fingers were shaking. So, if truth be told, was most of the rest of his body.

"What about Sandy?" he finally managed to ask.

For the first time, the man he trusted above all others seemed to hesitate.

"Dammit, Philip!" Alex felt like a man being stretched on a torture rack. One more turn and he would be broken.

"Elyssa Collins gave birth to a daughter six years ago last Sunday," Philip said, his tone no longer as even as it had been. "The baby was about eight weeks premature. There's no father listed on the birth certificate, Alex. But—" Again, he seemed to hesitate. A hint of sweat sheened the skin above his normally stiff upper lip.

"But, what?"

Philip looked Alex straight in the eye. "Sandy's given name is Alexandra Dawn."

How does a woman ask a man she's just made love with if he recalls going to bed with her more than six and a half years before?

How does a woman explain to that same man that even if they *were* lovers in the past, she has no memory of it . . . except in her dreams?

Those questions—and many others—tormented Elyssa as she prepared to return to Alex's apartment. The questions attacked her like angry hornets. Swarming. Stinging. A few she managed to swat away or evade. Most found vulnerable targets and inflicted hurt.

How does a woman tell a man he may be the father of her—

Bzzz.

Elyssa stiffened at the sudden shrill of her apartment's security intercom, her fingers freezing on the zipper of the pair of jeans she'd just pulled on. She knew, she absolutely knew, who was downstairs signalling her.

Bzzzzzz.

She zipped the jeans and tugged down the loose-fitting navy blue sweater she'd topped them with. She padded out of her small bedroom into the living room on bare feet, scarcely noticing when she stepped on a spoon from Sandy's new play kitchen.

Bzzzzzzzz.

The intercom was built into the foyer wall to the right of her front door. Elyssa flicked the control switch to Talk with unexpectedly steady fingers.

"Yes?" she asked. Her tone was as controlled as her hand had been.

"It's Alex."

She'd been prepared to hear his voice, of course. What she had not been prepared for was the surge of contradictory reactions she experienced when she did.

Embedded in the chaos of emotions erupting within her was one strangely compelling thought: *He came to find me. I left him and he came to find me.*

"Alex," she said aloud.

"Let me in, Elyssa."

Seven

"**I** know you must be angry," Elyssa found herself saying about a minute later. She'd thought she'd been braced for just about anything when she'd opened the door to admit Alex, but the expression on his lean-featured face was completely outside the realm of her experience. She felt a prickle of something close to fear when she registered his general dishevelment, then realized he was wearing the same shirt and trousers he'd had on the previous evening.

"Angry?" Alex echoed with a laugh that sounded like a knife blade being dragged over a whetstone. "Angry doesn't begin to describe what I am right now."

He stepped into the apartment without waiting for an invitation to enter, then brushed by Elyssa. He was desperate to put a little space between them. His mood was such at this moment that he genuinely didn't trust himself to be within touching distance of her.

Philip had tried to persuade him not to come here. Or, at least, to allow him to go along if he insisted on doing so. Alex had rejected his friend's entreaties without compunction. He'd waited too long to confront Elyssa as it was. He wasn't about to delay any further. He also wasn't about to say what he had to say, to do what he had to do, in front of a witness.

It was time for the truth. And the truth, in this case, involved just two people.

No, Alex corrected himself grimly. The truth, in this case, involved *three* people. Himself. Elyssa. And an innocent little girl named Alexandra Dawn.

His daughter, Alexandra Dawn.

Elyssa closed the front door of her apartment very carefully, then slowly followed Alex into her living room. There was an icy knot in her stomach that got tighter and colder with each step she took.

Alex was standing with his back to her, his head slightly bent. His broad shoulders were taut, straining against the wrinkled fabric of his white shirt. He had his hands jammed deep into the pockets of his trousers.

She came to a halt about three feet behind him. She saw his posture grow even stiffer, almost as though he expected her to stab him between the shoulder blades.

She drew a shaky breath, suddenly remembering the way he'd looked when she'd woken up beside him. Sleep had smoothed his features, erasing years and easing the harshness imposed by experience. He'd suddenly seemed vulnerable to her.

He seemed vulnerable now, too, but in a different and dangerous way. He reminded Elyssa of a wild, wounded tiger. Having been hurt, he would hurt back.

She wanted to turn and run but she didn't. She stood her ground and tried to find the right words to say.

"About last night—" she began unsteadily.

Alex pivoted to face her with the feral grace of a predator. "No," he said harshly. "We'll talk about last night . . . and this morning . . . in a few minutes. First we're going to talk about what happened between us six years and seven months ago on a Caribbean island called Corazón."

"Y-you?" Elyssa whispered, barely able to get the word out. Her breath wedged at the top of her throat. She had to struggle to force the single syllable around it.

"Yes, me," Alex affirmed, taking his hands out of his pockets. He was holding a thin black billfold. Elyssa watched him flip it open and extract what appeared to be a tattered photograph. "Me and you."

He held the snapshot out. After a few moments, Elyssa took it from him and stared down at a token of the past she thought had been lost to her forever.

What she saw in the water-stained photograph was a man and a woman gazing deep into each other's eyes. They were smiling as though they shared the secrets of the universe.

The man was Alexander Moran. Deeply tanned. Casually dressed. A rakish mustache riding the sensual line of his upper lip.

The woman was . . . herself. A honey-skinned version of herself wearing a sizzling fuchsia sarong and a spray of pink-frilled orchids.

She looked at Alex. "How long...how long have you had this?"

Alex took the photograph back and put it away, assessing her reaction. Her face was milk white and her lips were trembling. She seemed to be having trouble focusing.

"Since the day you vanished from Corazón," he finally replied.

"Since . . . since the day . . ."

Elyssa averted her gaze for several seconds, blinked rapidly, trying to absorb the implications of the photograph and Alex's possession of it. A thousand different thoughts careened through her brain, smashing into each other and splintering into pieces. She grasped at a fragment of one of the shattered thoughts and found it had a cutting edge.

He'd known. Alex had known and he hadn't said a word!

Blue eyes swung back and slammed into brown-gold ones.

"You knew," Elyssa said in an appalled tone. "All the time...from the very beginning...you knew. You knew who I was. You knew wh-what we'd d-done together..." She swallowed convulsively, shaking her head back and forth. "My God, you knew and you didn't say anything!"

The last thing in the world Alex had expected was an accusation. In his own mind, he was the wronged party in this situation. While he was dimly aware that this was not a very rational attitude, he didn't really care. She'd left him. *Twice* she'd left him!

Without stopping to consider the consequences, he lashed out.

"What was I supposed to say?" he demanded furiously. "'Hello, remember me? We had a fling a few years back. I'm the man you—'" He completed the sentence with an obscenity.

Elyssa's head snapped back as though he'd struck her across the face. In a few cruelly spoken syllables, Alex had confirmed all her worst fears about what she'd done on Isla de la Corazón.

"How could you!" she cried.

"The same way you could walk out on me this morning after last night," he retorted savagely.

The jump from past to present staggered her. "Last—last night?" she repeated thinly, then felt herself flush from breast to brow.

"Yes, last night." Alex caught Elyssa by the upper arms. "The two of us. Together. Naked. Needing. Wild with wanting each other." He gave her a little shake. "Or have you developed amnesia about that, too?"

"Amnesia?" She fought against his bruising grip and the tide of white-hot memories his explicit words had evoked. "How do you know about that?"

"I had you investigated," came the harsh reply.

"You *what?*" Elyssa's voice cracked. She went very still, staring at him with horrified eyes.

"After I found out about Sandy and realized she could be mine, I had you investigated," Alex elaborated, not bothering to add that he'd been investigating a woman he knew only as Dawn for well over six years. He then proceeded to summarize the information Philip had given him in four or five cold, concise sentences.

Elyssa moaned. She started to struggle again. "Let go of me!"

"No."

"Yes!" Twisting frantically, she managed to break his hold on her. She stepped back, her breath coming in short, shallow gasps. For years she'd been haunted by a dream.

Now that dream had become reality and it was a living nightmare.

"Elyssa—"

"Don't touch me!" She warded him off with a desperate gesture and took another step back. "I don't . . . I don't know what happened last night," she said raggedly. "I don't know why—"

"You don't know why you made love with me?" Alex cut in, his voice vibrant with rage. "You don't know why you took me so deep into your body—so deep I thought I'd die from the feel of it? You don't know why you came apart in my hands, crying my name—"

"Stop it!"

"Why?" He flung the word at her like a gauntlet. "You said you didn't know what happened last night. I'm trying to tell you. And I'll tell you what happened on Isla de la Corazón, too."

"*I don't want to hear it!*" Elyssa practically screamed at him.

There was a long and disasterous silence.

Alex watched Elyssa stumble over to the chintz-covered sofa about five feet from where they'd been standing. After collapsing onto it, she bent her head, her pale hair swinging forward to curtain her face. Despite the baggy fit of her dark blue sweater, it was obvious that the whole upper half of her body was shaking.

He didn't move. He wasn't at all sure he could.

Finally Elyssa lifted her head and looked at him. She was still very pale, visibly shuddering, but there was determination in the set of her finely molded features.

"What do you want, Alex?" she asked.

Alex caught his breath. Philip had asked him the same thing less than an hour earlier. After a moment, he gave Elyssa virtually the same answer he'd given his friend.

"I want what's mine," he replied flatly. "But I'll settle for another two weeks of your life."

Elyssa felt her heart turn over in her breast. "W-what?" she stammered.

"You and Sandy are going to come to Isla de la Corazón," he explained steadily. He wasn't proposing an idea.

He was presenting a fait accompli. "I have a place there. Two weeks will give me time to start to know my daughter. And maybe, just maybe, it will give you whatever it is you need to remember what happened between us as well."

"No." Elyssa shook her head, fiercely rejecting everything he'd just said.

"Yes."

"I can't."

"You will."

"Please..." Elyssa's voice trailed off as she watched Alex's expression harden and grow cold. "A-Alex?" she asked uncertainly.

"You and Sandy are going to come to Isla de la Corazón," he repeated. "You're going to stay with me, in my home. If you don't agree to this here and now, I'll claim paternity and file for custody of my daughter."

Six days later, Elyssa sat in one of the private departure lounges at John F. Kennedy International Airport waiting to board the jet that would take her on the first leg of her journey to Isla de la Corazón. Nikki Spears was slumped in a chair to her right, chasing down fistfuls of salted peanuts with gulps of vodka martini. Sandy was seated at a small table a few yards away. She was blissfully absorbed in a juice-and-cookie snack and a brand-new coloring book.

Elyssa plucked restlessly at the leather shoulder strap of her carry-on bag. Included in the contents of the tote was a pair of first-class airplane tickets charged to Alexander Moran. The tickets had been delivered to her at Carradine and Associates the morning after Alex had announced his ultimatum and she'd surrendered to it.

Elyssa glanced at her watch. Forty-four minutes to go. Approximately three minutes less than the last time she'd checked.

Forty-four minutes. Did she want those minutes to rush by, she wondered, or to drag on forever?

"Lmph, blzz—"

Elyssa started slightly, then turned to her right. "Nikki?"

Nikki swallowed the half-chewed peanuts that had distorted her speech, then took a quick sip of her drink. The three olives she'd specified when she'd ordered her martini from the lounge hostess bobbed in the bottom of the glass like miniature depth charges.

"Lys, please," she said in a tense undertone. "Listen to me. You don't have to do this."

Elyssa glanced toward her daughter. Sandy was scribbling industriously with a blue crayon. Her eyes were narrowed in an expression of artistic concentration, and the tip of her tongue was sticking out of one corner of her mouth.

Elyssa shifted her attention back to her friend. "Yes, Nikki," she responded quietly. "I do."

"No, you don't!" Nikki insisted. She had, for once, abandoned her basic black wardrobe. Pumpkin jersey studded with copper grommets was the fashion statement of the day. Unfortunately the impact of this vividly cheerful outfit was overshadowed by the bleakness of her expression and the grimness of her mood. Both were infinitely more gloomy than the contents of her closet had ever been.

"Nikki—"

"You can hire a lawyer. You can fight him!"

Elyssa shook her head emphatically, her hair swaying against her cheeks. She and Nikki had been over this same territory more than a dozen times during the past five days. The terrain did not improve with repetition.

"That's exactly what I'm trying to avoid," she told her friend, suppressing a shiver of anxiety. "No lawyers. No fighting. I don't want Sandy hurt."

"And you don't think this—this—*trip* is going to hurt her?" the brunette demanded.

Elyssa darted another look at her daughter. Sandy had apparently finished with the blue crayon. She was now busy drawing dots with a green one. From time to time she would pause to take a sip from the glass of apple juice at her elbow.

"No," she answered steadily, keeping her eyes on her little girl.

"And what about Alex Moran?"

Elyssa stiffened at the name, then turned to face her friend once again. "He won't hurt Sandy."

"Are you *sure*, Lys?" Nikki asked, leaning forward. "After what you said about the way he acted—are you sure?"

Elyssa met the brunette's urgent and unhappy gaze squarely. "Yes," she said quietly. "I'm sure."

She was telling the truth. One of the few things she was certain of at this point was that Alex Moran would not hurt his daughter. The mother of his daughter, perhaps, but not his daughter. If she'd had even the tiniest shred of doubt about that, she would have taken Sandy and fled.

There was a brief silence. Elyssa looked at her watch again.

Nikki tapped flame-colored fingernails against the arm of her chair. "Are you absolutely positive Alex Moran is Sandy's father?" she questioned bluntly.

Elyssa flushed. "Yes."

"She couldn't be what's-his-name's? Blaine? Dane?"

"Lane." Elyssa supplied, her sense of humiliation intensifying along with the hot color in her cheeks. "And no. She couldn't be. The timing's wrong. Besides," she paused, swallowing hard, "Lane always took precautions."

"There couldn't have been someone else? I mean, you've got a gap in your memory—"

"Nikki!" Elyssa gasped, too appalled to keep her voice down. She glanced anxiously over her shoulder at Sandy. She breathed a prayer of thanks when she saw that her daughter was totally engrossed in licking the icing out of the middle of a cream-filled cookie. After a moment, she turned back to her friend.

"All right, all right." The brunette dipped her head, clearly conceding she'd gone over the line with her last question. "I'm sorry, Lys. It's just that this whole situation is so...so..." She gestured expansively.

"Yes, I know," Elyssa said, smiling wanly.

Nikki heaved a heavy sigh. "I wish you'd told me before."

"I couldn't."

"But you shouldn't have had to carry all this around inside you for so many years with no help! I always thought you were gutsy—"

"Me? Gutsy?" Elyssa interrupted, startled by the description.

Her friend nodded emphatically. "Yes, gutsy. Going it alone the way you have. Working. Raising Sandy. Forget about hanging Purple Hearts on paratroopers. I think single mothers are the ones who should get medals for valor."

Elyssa was touched but not quite ready to accept her friend's admiration. She was all too conscious of her failures of strength and courage. "I wasn't very gutsy when you talked to me on Sunday," she observed ruefully, hooking a lock of hair behind one ear.

Nikki grimaced. "For God's sake!" she expostulated. "I phoned you—what? Fifteen minutes after Alexander Moran left? You'd just been hit with the emotional equivalent of a hydrogen bomb! Most people I know would have been gargling razor blades or worse."

"I'm glad you decided to come over."

"There was no way I was going to let you be alone, Lys. I just wish there'd been something constructive I could have done."

"You listened."

"You mean, I sat there with my mouth hanging open like an idiot while you told me the most incredible story I'd ever heard in my life."

"I mean, *you listened,*" Elyssa repeated, remembering how she'd finally poured out the truth to her friend. "And it helped. It really did help, Nikki. Having you here now helps, too. Believe me."

There was another break in their conversation. Elyssa used the pause to check on Sandy once again. The little girl had gone back to crayoning. She was hunched over her coloring book, her ribbon-tied braids trailing down her back.

Elyssa suppressed a sigh. She'd struggled hard to hide the emotional turmoil she was experiencing from her daughter. So far, her efforts appeared to be paying off. For this, she was deeply grateful.

Sandy had accepted the news of their impending trip to Isla de la Corazón with astonishing aplomb. She was excited by the prospect, but not overly so. Her only anxieties seemed to be that their plane might be "hij-napped" by "pirates" or that the waters around the island where they were going might be filled with sharks.

As for her reaction to word that they would be staying with the man she called "Mr. M'ran"...

There was, in truth, only one way to describe her reaction. From the very start, Sandy had behaved as though spending a vacation with Alexander Moran was the most natural thing in the world. Her greatest disappointment was that he'd gone ahead to the island instead of flying there with her.

Mr. M'ran, Sandy had confided to her mother, would have been able to beat up any and all would-be plane pirates. He could probably beat up sharks, too, if he really tried.

"Lys?"

Elyssa turned back to Nikki. "Yes?"

"What do you think's going to happen once you get to the island?"

Elyssa considered this question for several moments then said honestly, "I don't know, Nikki. But whatever it is, I'm willing to face it. I have to."

"And if there's a storm?"

Elyssa felt her cheeks grow warm. She'd told her friend about her dreams, too. Oddly enough, Nikki had seemed more stunned by that revelation than by anything else.

"If there's a storm, I won't go to sleep," she responded, smoothing her palm against the khaki cotton slacks she was wearing.

"You weren't asleep last Saturday night."

"No, I wasn't," Elyssa conceded after a few seconds.

"But you still..." Nikki paused with uncharacteristic delicacy.

Elyssa shook her head, avoiding the brunette's questioning gaze. "I don't know what happened last Saturday," she said tightly, then amended, "I mean, I do know.

I . . . remember. I remember what I did. I remember what Alex did."

"He didn't force you?"

Elyssa looked at her friend, genuinely shocked. "No, Nikki. Oh, God, n-no." Her voice wavered as a flood of memories washed through her brain. Her body began to hum in response to the intensely erotic images. "I—I wanted—"

"Ah, excuse me," a male voice interrupted. "Are you Elyssa Collins?"

Elyssa started. Turning in her seat, she looked up into the face of a man who was a complete stranger to her. He was of medium height and build and had dark blond hair and blue-gray eyes. His clothing exuded the ageless elegance of custom tailoring. Despite a hint of awkwardness in his manner, he projected an aura of calm and compassion.

Elyssa's eyes slewed briefly toward her daughter. Sandy was now proudly displaying her coloring project to one of the departure lounge hostesses. She returned her attention to the unknown man.

"Yes, I am," she confirmed warily.

The stranger offered her a smile that clearly was meant to reassure. "I'm Philip Lassiter," he introduced himself.

Elyssa stiffened with alarm. "Alex's lawyer?"

"Lawyer?" Nikki echoes sharply, sitting bolt upright.

Philip's blue-gray eyes bounced from Elyssa to Nikki and back again. "You know who I am?"

Elyssa nodded once. A dozen different explanations for this man's presence popped into her head. None of them was pleasant.

"Exactly what are you doing here?" Nikki demanded. Her tone suggested that Philip Lassiter was about as welcome as a slug in a salad.

Elyssa saw the lawyer's gaze shift back and forth again and knew he was trying to figure out Nikki's connection to her. Under different circumstances, she would have been amused by his obvious puzzlement. She was well aware that she and Nikki probably appeared to people to be the most unlikely of friends.

Almost as unlikely, she thought suddenly, as this man and Alexander Moran.

Elyssa cleared her throat. "Mr. Lassiter, this is my friend, Nicole Spears," she said. "She's seeing Sandy and me off today. Nikki, this is Philip Lassiter. Alex Moran's lawyer...and best friend."

Philip was plainly surprised by this last designation. After a moment, he extended his hand to Nikki. "How do you do, Ms. Spears," he said courteously.

Nikki folded her arms across her chest. "Frankly, I don't do very well, Mr. Lassiter," she returned. "And Elyssa—who happens to be *my* best friend, by the way—is probably doing a lot worse than I am."

Philip slowly brought his hand back down to his side. "I see."

"Oh, do you?" Nikki parried.

Elyssa patted her friend's arm, wordlessly urging restraint. Despite her initial surge of fear, there was something about this man that told her he was trustworthy.

"Mr. Lassiter, why are you here?" she questioned.

Philip seemed to have trouble dragging his gaze away from Nikki. "Ah, well," he began uneasily, finally managing to turn his eyes back to Elyssa. He cleared his throat and tugged on his tie. "Since, ah, Alex went on ahead to Corazón, he asked me to come out to the airport today to—ah—ah—"

"To make sure Elyssa and Sandy actually get on the plane?" Nikki suggested scathingly. "That makes you—what? An accomplice to blackmail?"

"Nikki—"

"Actually, Ms. Spears," Philip cut in, his tone turning steely, "it makes me a man who's been placed in an extremely uncomfortable position." He looked squarely at Elyssa and declared, "Alex wanted to be certain everything went smoothly for you and...Sandy."

"That's very considerate, Mr. Lassiter," Elyssa responded after a moment, wondering about the way the lawyer had hesitated before he'd spoken Sandy's name. "Thank you."

Nikki snorted.

Philip's shoulders went rigid beneath his impeccably styled navy suit jacket. "You're welcome, Ms. Collins," he replied evenly. "As I said, I've been placed in an extremely uncomfortable position. There's something I'd very much like you to know. I definitely do not approve of what Alex is doing in this situation."

"I'm sure all lawyers say that when their clients start coercing people," Nikki sniped nastily.

"Nikki, please!"

"I don't approve of what he's doing as an attorney or as a friend," Philip clarified, shooting Nikki a quelling look. "But I do understand it. Or, at least, I think I do."

Elyssa found herself leaning forward. "Mr. Lassiter—"

"Do you mind if I sit down, Ms. Collins?" he interrupted, forking his fingers through his neatly brushed hair in an agitated manner.

Elyssa was struck by the urgency of Philip's request. It was clear he was deeply upset. "No. Of course not," she said quietly, ignoring an unmistakable sound of protest from Nikki.

"Thank you." Philip seated himself, spine straight, shoulders squared. He opened his mouth as though intending to speak, then shut it again. He stayed silent for nearly fifteen seconds.

"Mr. Lassiter?" Elyssa prompted.

Philip sighed and met her gaze. "Look, I don't know exactly what happened between you and Alex last weekend," he said slowly. "He literally ran into me Sunday in the lobby of his apartment. I gather he was...going after you. He didn't want to stop. The only reason he did was because I told him I had the summary of the background investigation he'd ordered done on you." He paused, lifting his brows questioningly.

"I know about that," Elyssa confirmed a bit stiffly.

"Ah. I see." Philip nodded, then cleared his throat before continuing. "Once I got done telling Alex what the agency had learned, he left and went to you. As I said, I don't know exactly what transpired. But I do know Alex wasn't in a very rational state. Because of this, I think he probably said or did some things when he was with you that he now regrets. The problem is, having said and done them, he can't find a way of taking them back." Philip gestured with both hands, his expression grave. "Ms. Collins, I realize this situation is terribly difficult for you. But Alex ... well, Alex has been suffering for a long time."

"Oh, give me a break!" Nikki exploded furiously. "Do you have any idea what Elyssa's been through? She woke up in a hospital room with no memory of two weeks of her life. A month later she found out she was pregnant. She was all alone, Mr. Lassiter! She didn't hear one word from your friend and client for more than six and a half years. For that alone, Alexander Moran deserves the worst kind of—"

"My God," Philip interrupted in a stunned voice. Although his gaze had shifted to Nikki when she'd started her diatribe, he was now staring at Elyssa. His expression was one of appalled comprehension. "You don't know."

His words—and the way he said them—touched off a strange sensation deep inside Elyssa. "I don't know what?" she asked.

"He didn't tell you," Philip went on, acting as though he hadn't heard her inquiry. He slammed his hand against the chair he was sitting in. "Dammit! Alex didn't tell you!"

"Alex didn't tell me *what?*" Elyssa questioned sharply.

Philip blinked, then focused on her as though rediscovering her presence. When he spoke, his voice was taut with suppressed emotion.

"Ms. Collins," he said, "Alex has been trying to find you ever since he came back from Isla de la Corazón after the hurricane. He's had investigators looking for you for more than six years." He darted a quick look at Nikki. "And if you doubt my word, I can supply you with monthly reports from the detective agency he hired."

Elyssa clenched her hands and brought them to her breast. Her heart was pounding. She felt faint.

"It couldn't have been a very good detective agency," she heard Nikki comment across a great distance. The roar of her blood in her ears made it difficult to understand exactly what her friend was saying. "I mean, how many Elyssa Collinses from Chicago can there be?"

"Alex didn't know Elyssa Collins from Chicago," Philip answered with devastating simplicity. His blue-gray eyes were grim. "The woman he met on Corazón told him her name was Dawn. That's about *all* she told him."

Eight

It was almost sunset when the twin-engine plane carrying Elyssa and Sandy appeared in the cloudless sky over the small airstrip on the north end of Isla de la Corazón. The plane was nearly thirty minutes late. Going by "island" standards, that qualified as being right on time.

Alex had driven to the landing field from his home on the south end of the island. He'd come early because the charter service that flew in and out of Corazón was as notorious for running ahead of schedule as behind it. He'd wanted to be certain to be on hand when Elyssa and Sandy arrived.

Philip had phoned several hours before to recount what had happened in the departure lounge at Kennedy Airport. Until that call, Alex had believed that the discoveries he'd made about Elyssa's amnesia and Sandy's paternity had rendered him immune to being shocked or infuriated by the twists and turns of fate. The story his friend had related had proven he was wrong.

Alex leaned back against the battered but dependable Jeep he'd come in and closed his eyes, replaying the conversation in his head.

"She thought *what?*" he'd demanded.

"You heard me the first time, Alex," Philip had countered, the edge in his voice coming through loud and clear despite the crackle of static on the line. "My God, what was she supposed to think? She woke up in a hospital with a two-week gap in her memory. A month later she discovered she was going to have a baby. She had no idea who the father was. No idea about the circumstances of conception. In the meantime, no one had tried to contact her—"

"So she jumped to the conclusion she'd gotten pregnant because of a sleazy one-night stand with some stranger who didn't give a damn?"

"Yes," his friend had affirmed succinctly. "That's the impression I got."

It was then that Alex had remembered the phrase he'd flung at Elyssa in her apartment less than a week before. With sickening clarity, he'd recalled how he'd used an obscenity to describe what had gone on between them on Isla de la Corazón. He'd also recalled the shattered look he'd seen in Elyssa's expressive blue eyes after he'd said the word.

He hadn't meant it. Dear Lord, he hadn't meant it! What he'd experienced on Corazón had been the very antithesis of obscenity and he knew it. He'd known it even as he'd spit out the word. But it hadn't mattered. Elyssa had hurt him. He'd wanted to hurt her back. So, goaded by pain and anger, he'd lashed out in the cruelest way he could think of.

But he'd never dreamed she might actually believe...

"Oh, God, Philip," he groaned into the telephone mouthpiece, loathing himself for what he'd said and done.

"It may be all right, Alex," Philip had responded. "She knows the truth now."

"The truth?"

"She knows you looked for her."

"She knows I didn't find her."

"I explained about your having nothing but the name 'Dawn' to go on."

"And did she explain why that's all she told me?"

Philip had stayed silent for several seconds. "I gather that's one of the things she can't remember," he'd answered eventually.

"So, she *doesn't* know the truth."

"For the love of—" the man on the other end of the line had sputtered. "At least she knows more of the truth than she did. Dammit, Alex! Why didn't you tell her you'd been searching for her ever since you were separated? Why didn't you tell her the first time you saw her again? *Why didn't you tell her who you were?*"

"Because I didn't know what to say, Philip."

"Well, figure it out," his friend had counseled trenchantly.

Alex opened his eyes. The plane had touched down on the landing strip and was now taxiing slowly in his direction. Taking a deep breath, he pushed himself away from the Jeep.

Figure out what to say, he told himself.

Then figure out how to say it . . . and when.

"I see him, Mommy!" Sandy exclaimed, pressing her nose against the small window next to her seat. "I see Mr. M'ran!"

"Do you?" Elyssa responded. The pilot had just shut down the engines. The four other passengers on the tiny aircraft were already scrambling for the exit.

"Uh-huh, uh-huh," Sandy confirmed, bouncing up and down. A second later she started waving. "Now he sees me!" she reported in delighted tone.

"Oh...good," Elyssa said, unbuckling her seat belt with carefully controlled fingers. She then reached over and undid her daughter's seat belt, too.

"Let's get off!" Sandy urged, turning away from the window. Her brown eyes were fizzy with anticipation, her soft cheeks flushed with excitement.

"Just a second," Elyssa answered, leaning forward to retrieve her carry-on tote. The fingers that had been so steady only a moment before started to shake. She bit her lip, struggling to still the trembling.

She'd spent most of the past six days preparing herself for this impending moment of return and reunion. She'd even reached the point where she honestly believed she was ready for it. When she'd told Nikki she was willing to face whatever waited for her on Isla de la Corazón, she'd been speaking the truth.

But barely five minutes after she'd uttered that truth, Philip Lassiter had blown nearly all the assumptions it was based on to bits. Elyssa was still reeling from the revelations he'd made. It seemed the more she learned about her relationship with Alex, the less she understood.

If only she could remember what had gone on between them! She was sick and tried of trying to piece together the two most crucial weeks of her life from secondhand fragments. She needed to find out exactly what had happened on Isla de la Corazón. She needed to discover it for herself. . . and by herself.

She needed to do a great many things.

"Mom-my!" Sandy's voice had an edge to it. The elbow she poked into Elyssa's ribs was fairly sharp, too. "Mr. M'ran's waiting for us!"

The first of those things was to get herself off the plane and face Alex Moran again.

Mine, Alex thought fiercely when Sandy appeared in the door of the plane.

His, but he couldn't claim her. At least, not yet. Maybe never.

Mine, too, Alex thought even more fiercely when Elyssa materialized behind the little girl a moment later.

He knew he couldn't claim her now, either. Not after the things he'd said and done.

His little girl was smiling and waving at him. Her mother was not.

Alex began walking forward. He waved, but he didn't smile.

"Hi, Mr. M'ran!" Sandy called, bounding down the plane's rickety metal exit steps on small, sneakered feet.

"Hello, Sandy," he called back. Hello, Alexandra Dawn, he added silently.

When they'd spoken on the phone earlier, Philip had sworn he'd detected a definite resemblance between father and daughter. But try as he might now, Alex couldn't see more than a vague similarity in coloring.

His assessment was much different when he shifted his gaze from Sandy's face to Elyssa's. They seemed remarkably alike to him. In Sandy, he saw intimations of the child Elyssa must once have been. In Elyssa, he glimpsed the promise of the woman Sandy would one day become.

The little girl darted across the tarmac to him. Surrendering to impulse, Alex scooped her up. He was rewarded with a quick hug. Then Sandy started a chattering comparison of the "big" plane that had flown her from New York to Florida and the "baby" one that had brought her to Isla de la Corazón.

Alex didn't register much of what she was saying. The realization that he was holding his daughter in his arms for the first time compelled most of his attention. Elyssa's graceful approach commanded the rest.

They look so much alike, Elyssa thought poignantly, walking toward her only child and the man who had fathered her. She wondered how she could have failed to notice the resemblance earlier. It was more than a matter of virtually identical coloring. More than a similar angularity of features. It was the cock of their heads, the quick intelligence in their eyes . . . oh, Lord, they even smiled in the same crook-cornered way!

She felt a sharp, sudden urge to snatch Sandy away from Alex and hug her close. She'd never shared her little girl with anyone. She'd carried her in her body—alone. She'd raised her—alone. Sandy was *her* daughter!

But she was Alex's daughter, too. That was something Elyssa couldn't deny. Alexander Moran was Sandy's father.

He was also the man she now knew had spent more than six and a half years looking for a woman called Dawn.

Elyssa came to a halt about two feet from Alex, asking herself what those years of searching must have been like for him. She also asked herself what he must feel about the outcome of all that effort. Yes, he'd discovered a daughter he hadn't known he had, a daughter he was obviously prepared to acknowledge and embrace. But the true purpose of

his quest had not been accomplished. He hadn't found
Dawn.

He'd found her, Elyssa Collins, instead.

She—Elyssa Collins—was not the lover Alexander Moran
had known so intimately on Corazón. She recognized that.
She had no doubt that he'd recognized it, too. She was not
the smiling, sensual young woman in the tattered photograph Alex had carried with him for so long.

For one painful instant, all she could think about was how
bitterly disappointed he must be.

"Hello, Elyssa," Alex said quietly, observing the play of
emotion across her features. Resentment. Anxiety. Hurt.
Sadness. He saw them all and knew he was responsible.

"Hello, Alex," Elyssa responded. She sustained his gaze
for several moments, then averted her eyes and began to
glance around. She was conscious of a tightness in her chest
and throat.

This is Isla de la Corazón, she told herself. I've been here
before. There must be something familiar about it. There
must be something—a sight, a sound, a smell—I remember. *Something!*

Alex watched Elyssa survey her surroundings. He saw the
smooth skin of her forehead pleat and the rosy fullness of
her lips thin. He sensed her searching . . . straining . . . and
realized what she was trying to do. He also realized it would
serve little purpose in this particular place.

"This airstrip is new," he commented casually, setting
Sandy back on her feet. The little girl took a hop-skip over
to her mother and grasped her hand.

Elyssa looked back at Alex. She was shaken by the compassion she glimpsed in the gold-flecked depths of his brown
eyes. "You mean it wasn't here when—" she hesitated,
darting an anxious look at Sandy.

"No," he answered quickly. "It wasn't."

A warm breeze ruffled Elyssa's hair. She raised her free
hand and smoothed it down. "I suppose the island has
changed over the years."

Alex's mouth twisted. "A lot of things have."

* * *

Four hours later, Elyssa walked slowly onto the terrace of the elegant island villa that would be her home for the next two weeks. She'd just finished putting her daughter to bed in a lovely white and coral room that looked out on a silver sand beach and the moonlit waters of the Caribbean.

"Is everything all right?" Alex asked. He'd been leaning against the terrace's wooden railing, toying with a palm frond for nearly thirty minutes. At Elyssa's appearance, he straightened and discarded the leaf. He was acutely aware that this was the first time he and she had been alone together since their confrontation in her apartment.

"Everything's fine." She met Alex's dark gaze for a few seconds, then glanced away, inhaling deeply. The evening air was heady with the scent of flowers.

"You were gone a long time."

Elyssa shifted her weight and fiddled with the embroidered tie belt of the gauzy white dress she'd changed into after arriving at the villa. She heard genuine concern in Alex's voice. She also heard a hint of something else she wasn't certain how to interpret.

"It took me a while to get Sandy settled down," she responded. This was true, as far as it went. What it left unsaid was that she'd been infinitely more lenient with her daughter's bedtime stalling tactics this particular evening than she'd ever been in the past. She was honest enough with herself to admit that she'd been indulging in a few stalling tactics of her own.

"Too keyed up to go to sleep?"

"Something like that." After a few moments, she moved to stand within a few feet of him. Bracing her palms on the terrace railing, she stared out at the silver-dappled sea. Should I know this place? she wondered, her pulse fluttering. Was this where—?

Alex saw Elyssa's profile fret suddenly, much as it had at the air-strip. He experienced a sharp stab of remorse. When he'd spoken to her six days before about the possibility that a return to Corazón would restore her memory, he'd never considered the kind of torment he might be forcing her to undergo. He tried for a moment to put himself in her place.

Tried to imagine what it would be like to come to a place knowing he'd been there, knowing it had played a pivotal part in his life, but having no recollection of it.

It was not a pleasant feeling.

"You were never here, Elyssa," he told her quietly.

She turned her head to look at him, unnerved by his apparent ability to track the path of her thoughts. "No?" she asked, the word catching briefly in her throat.

"No. I bought this property about five years ago."

Elyssa gripped the railing, gazing out at the sea once again. Her reaction to the information she'd just been given was an unsettling combination of relief and regret.

The source of the relief was easy to pinpoint. As much as Elyssa wanted to learn what had happened to her on Corazón, something inside her shied from the idea of following too closely in Dawn's footsteps in order to do so. *She wasn't Dawn.*

The reason for the regret was more complex. She'd been drawn to the villa the instant they'd driven up to it in Alex's Jeep. Flanked by bearded fig trees and travelers' palms and surrounded by a lush profusion of flowering plants, the elegantly simple white structure had beckoned to her with a special kind of warmth. While it would not be correct to say she'd felt as though she'd come home, she had had an immediate sense of belonging. It was a far cry from her initial reaction to Alex's New York apartment.

Having been at the villa before would have helped her explain her affinity for the place. But it seemed her response was rooted in the present, not the past.

Elyssa drew a shaky breath. The sweetly perfumed air hazed her brain for a moment. Oleander. Bougainvillea. Frangipani.

And orchids. Dainty, delicate, pink-frilled orchids. The ride from the airstrip had shown her that such orchids grew all over Isla de la Corazón. It had obviously been no accident that Alex had sent her such flowers the day after they'd met.

Somewhere...
Sometime...

He'd known. From the very beginning, he'd known. And he hadn't said a word.

"Why didn't you tell me, Alex?" Elyssa asked abruptly, turning her head to look at him once again. Her fair hair rippled about her throat.

"Tell you what?"

"Anything." She gestured. "Everything. Why didn't you tell me who you were? That first day at Moranco—why didn't you say something?"

Now Alex was the one to stare out at the moonlit sea. "Philip asked me the same question this afternoon."

Elyssa moistened her lips with a quick dart of her tongue. "You spoke to Philip?"

"Yes."

"Then you know what I found out from him."

"And what he found out from you."

A few seconds went by.

"Why, Alex?" Elyssa repeated. "Please. Tell me why. Tell me the truth."

He brought his eyes back to meet hers. Figure out what to say, he told himself as he had earlier. Then figure out how to say it . . . and when.

"Pride was a big part of it," he admitted after pause.

"Pride?"

He nodded, hearing the surprise in her voice, seeing the puzzlement in her face. He gave himself several moments to marshall his thoughts, hoping he would be able to say what he needed to say in the way it needed to be said. When he began speaking, his voice was very level and carefully controlled.

"Imagine a man who has ten days in paradise with one special woman then loses her," he said slowly. "Imagine him spending the next six and a half years searching for her. He doesn't know what happened to her. Where she is. Who she's with. Lord, he doesn't even know whether she's alive or dead! So he hopes. And prays. He makes a lot of money and a lot of noise so that if she's searching for him, he'll be very easy to locate. He wakes up every morning dreaming. He goes to bed every night disappointed. And then, late one afternoon, he walks into a conference room and there she is.

The woman he's been looking for. For a moment he thinks he may have gone crazy. He's afraid he's wanted this one thing so much, for so long, that he's finally snapped. Then the fear passes and he accepts that the woman is real. *He's found her.* And for a few seconds, he's in paradise again. But then he realizes that the woman—his woman—is looking at him as though he's a stranger. As though they've never met before. She smiles, exactly the way he remembers her smiling. It's part sweet, part shy, with a tiny touch of seductiveness she doesn't even know about, and it makes his heart stop for a beat or two. She shakes his hand. That one touch makes him ache. Then she says something to him. Something polite. Something impersonal.''

He stopped, clenching and unclenching his hands. His entire body was tense. He could feel the rigidity of muscles and sinew as he struggled to channel the emotional anguish that was pouring through him like a river of acid. When he spoke again, his voice was rough.

"In other words," he went on, "this one special woman treats this man exactly the way she's treated God knows how many other men God knows how many other times. And it hurts. It hurts his pride. His manhood. Whatever you want to call it. It hurts like hell."

Elyssa stared at him, stunned by the dark force of his words. While she'd had some hint about the depth of Alex's feeling from Philip Lassiter, nothing the lawyer had said at the airport had prepared her for what she'd just heard.

"Oh, Alex," she whispered, trembling a little. "I didn't know. I didn't realize. If only—"

"It's not your fault," he cut her off harshly. "It's nobody's fault."

There was another pause. Alex looked back out to sea. Elyssa studied him silently. The moonlight had leeched most of the color out of his face, reducing his features to silver-brushed planes and shadowed hollows. The strength he'd been endowed with was plain in every compelling line. So was the stress he was under.

She was suddenly shaken by an impulse to close the distance between them. She wanted to move to him and put her arms around him. She wanted to feel his arms come around her in return. They'd caused each other so much pain, she thought. Knowingly. Unknowingly. Perhaps they could offer each other some basic human—

"Don't," Alex warned. The single syllable shattered the silence the way a dropped rock shatters a pane of glass.

Elyssa froze, realizing with a shock that she'd taken a step forward. Her need to go to him had been so powerful, she acted on it without thinking about what she was doing.

"No pity," he said. His voice was as cold and spiked as ice-covered barbed wire.

She shook her head, denying his reading of her motivation. "Alex, I wasn't—"

He faced her, his eyes flashing gold. "Yes, you were, Elyssa. You were feeling sorry that you'd hurt me. Don't. My wounded pride was only part of what kept me from saying anything to you. The other part was that I couldn't completely accept the idea you'd forgotten me. A matter of pride, too, I suppose. The fact is, I thought you might be putting on an act."

It took Elyssa a few seconds to assimilate this statement. She was still deeply disturbed by his characterization of her response to what he'd told her, but every instinct she had told her not to pursue it.

She swallowed hard. "What made you think that?"

"The way you responded to me."

Elyssa flushed. "You mean . . . when you kissed me."

Alex's eyes slid over her, seeming to strip away the light fabric of her dress. She shifted her weight from one foot to the other, remembering the electric sense of connection she'd had when their hands had touched for what she'd believed was the first time. He'd said that brief moment of contact had made him ache.

It had made her burn.

"Even before that," he said.

Elyssa let a few moments go by. "I still don't understand why you'd think I'd pretend not to know you if I did."

"You said you were a widow."

She stiffened at the reminder of the lies she'd told him. "Yes," she conceded. "But why—"

"Before I found out the truth, I thought you might have been married when we were together on Corazón," he interrupted with devastating bluntness. He knew there were gentler ways to explain, but he wasn't going to give her gentleness at this moment. He wanted Elyssa to understand that no matter how battered and bloody his emotions might be, he didn't need offers of solace from anyone. "I thought you might have committed adultery with me while you were carrying your husband's child. I also thought it was possible you might have gotten pregnant by me but convinced your husband the baby was his. Either one of those scenarios would explain why you'd prefer not to admit knowing me."

Alex's words hit Elyssa like a bucket of ice water. "You—you believed—?"

"What about what you believed?" he countered sharply, then found himself assailed by the same kind of shame he'd experienced earlier when he'd spoken with Philip. He forced himself to go on. "I saw your expression six days ago when I called what happened between us a fling—and worse. You were ready to accept my description, Elyssa. Don't deny it."

The obscenity he'd used echoed through Elyssa's brain. No, she thought painfully. She couldn't deny it. She had been ready to accept what he'd said as the truth. Based on what she'd known and felt then, she'd been more than willing to believe the ugly picture he'd painted of what they'd done together.

"I had good reason," she defended herself.

"Well, so did I," he returned.

Elyssa went pale and stepped back. "You did?"

It took Alex a second to sort out her reaction. He'd been talking about having had good reason for believing what he'd believed. He realized with a jolt that she must have thought he'd been referring to the cruel words he'd thrown at her in her apartment.

"No, Elyssa," he said quickly, compellingly. "Oh, God, no. There was no reason for my saying that."

Elyssa tilted her chin slightly. "Then why did you?"

"I was angry."

"Because...I'd left you." She wondered fleetingly if she'd ever be able to tell him she'd been on her way back to him when he'd arrived at her apartment. She also wondered if he'd believe her if she did.

"Because you'd left me for the second time."

Elyssa's lips parted with a rush of breath. "The second time?"

Alex nodded. He'd gone this far, he might as well go the whole way. "You left me on Corazón. After the hurricane."

Shock momentarily deprived Elyssa of the ability to speak. For a moment, the terrace seemed to tilt beneath her feet. She grasped onto the railing as though it were a lifeline.

"Wh-what?" she finally choked out. "How can you possibly feel—my Lord, Alex! You *know* what happened to me. You know what happened to me better than I do!"

"I don't expect you to think it's rational," he responded tightly, forking his fingers back through his hair. His hand wasn't quite steady. "God, even I don't think it's rational. But you said you wanted the truth. The truth is that for more than six and a half years, I've had this little voice reminding me you said you'd be somewhere waiting for me and you weren't. And when I woke up last Sunday morning and you weren't there again . . ."

Alex let his voice trail off, wishing he could block the memory of the moment when he'd realized he was alone in his apartment.

"Déjà vu," Elyssa suggested in a strange voice. Her initial spurt of outrage had faded. In its place had come the feeling that she'd just had several important pieces of a complicated puzzle slotted into place for her. Unfortunately the pattern she sensed emerging was not one she wanted to contemplate.

Alex felt a flash of surprise. He'd expected Elyssa to throw his semi-coherent explanation back in his face. Lord knew, she had every right to. But instead of the rebuff he'd been braced to receive, he saw a glimmer of understanding in her eyes.

"Something like that," he agreed warily.

"And after you'd found out the truth? After Philip told you what the investigators had learned?"

He gestured, his expression turning grim. "You were there, Elyssa. You saw. You heard."

Elyssa averted her head, gazing at the sea once again but not really seeing it. There was a peculiar logic to the feelings Alex had admitted, she thought, even if he didn't seem to recognize them.

Alex's father had abandoned him when he was a toddler. His mother had died when he was in his teens. Those two events had obviously scarred him very deeply. Sometimes such scarring numbed a person's ability to feel. In Alex's case, the wounds he'd suffered apparently had made him extremely vulnerable to the pain of being rejected or deserted. To lead a solitary life by choice was one thing. But to be left alone because of someone else's doing was entirely another.

Elyssa knew, from bitter personal experience, the kind of anger emotional loss could generate. It had taken her years to realize how much rage she'd felt because of her father's death. It had taken her even longer to realize that much of that rage had been directed at her beloved and blameless parent.

The truth is that for more than six and a half years, I've had this little voice reminding me you said you'd be somewhere waiting for me and you weren't. And when I woke up last Sunday morning and you weren't there again...

Alex had a right to be angry about the way she'd snuck out of his apartment, Elyssa acknowledged. She was going to have to find the courage to explain what she knew was an act of cowardice to him, and to herself.

As for his anger about the circumstances that had kept them apart for more than six and a half years...

No, she corrected herself. Not the circumstances that had kept *them* apart. The circumstances that had kept him and *Dawn* apart. That was what Alex was angry about. That and the discovery that he'd been cheated out of the first six years of his daughter's life. And she—she, Elyssa—had become the target for his anger.

Alex had kept saying "you" to her a few minutes before. But Elyssa knew he'd really meant Dawn. After all, it had been Dawn who'd been with him on Corazón. And it had been Dawn he'd expected to wake up with six days before because it had been Dawn he'd made love to during the Saturday night storm.

Hadn't it?

"Elyssa?" Alex questioned.

She turned and looked at him. "I'm here," was all she said.

Nine

"**P**sssst."

A hissing sound and the sensation of being stared at drew Elyssa out of a deep and dreamless slumber late the next morning. A small finger nudged gently at her shoulder, urging her along the road to full consciousness. She stirred restlessly.

"Psssst." A puff of breath—as warm and soft as a kitten's paw—skimmed over her cheek. "Psssst."

"Mmmph," Elyssa muttered vaguely.

"Mommy," a sweet little voice whispered with just a touch of irritation, "are you done sleeping yet?"

Elyssa felt another poke at her shoulder. It was a bit more insistent than the previous one. After a moment, her lashes fluttered open and she found herself looking directly into her daughter's face.

Sandy's freckle-dusted nose was less than a foot away from hers. The little girl was hunkered down beside the bed Elyssa was lying in, her pointed chin resting on the edge of the mattress. Her glossy brown hair had been inexpertly braided into a pair of pigtails. The one on the left side was noticeably fatter and higher than the one on the right, and the part on the top of her head was decidedly crooked.

Elyssa felt disoriented. Her gaze drifted over surroundings that were only vaguely familiar. White-washed walls. Wicker and natural wood furniture with aqua and white upholstery. Floor-to-ceiling windows hung with sheer, breeze-stirred white curtains.

"Sandy?" she questioned throatily, not quite certain she was awake.

"Hi, mommy!" Sandy responded in a cheery tone. The smile that lit her face was brighter than a sunbeam. She scrambled to her feet, pigtails swinging merrily. "I *knew* it was time for you to wake up. Mr. M'ran said maybe not, but I knew it was."

The words "Mr. M'ran" swept through Elyssa's brain like a strong wind, blowing down all the cobwebs. Her sleep-induced fuzziness fled. Reality snapped sharply into focus.

Memories of the night before rushed in. What Alex had said. What she'd said. The way they'd parted company shortly after their exchange about his anger over her leaving him. The way she'd tossed and turned for hours after she'd gone to her room . . . very much alone.

Elyssa levered herself up on one elbow. Fair hair spilled forward to veil her eyes. She tossed her head to clear her face. The strap of her white cotton nightgown slipped off her right shoulder. She shrugged it back into place. Instincts that had been lying dormant less than a minute before quivered to life, clamoring an alarm.

"Sandy—" she began.

But Sandy had already skipped away from the bed and across the room's white tile floor. In the same instant Elyssa finished saying her name, she flung open the bedroom door.

"See?" Sandy sang out triumphantly, staring up at the tall, dark-haired man standing in the doorway. She gestured back toward Elyssa. "I *told* you it was time for mommy to be awake."

"So you did, Sandy," Alexander Moran replied genially, flashing the little girl a smile and a wink.

Elyssa maneuvered herself into a sitting position, struggling to maintain both her balance and her dignity. She clutched the sheets against her with one hand and scooped her hair back from her brow with the other. The rhythm of her pulse had gone from steady to syncopated in a matter of seconds. She stared at the man who held the key to her past . . . and, quite possibly, her future.

Alex was wearing a torso-hugging white T-shirt and a pair of ancient denim cutoffs that looked as though they'd been spray painted on. His feet were bare, his dark hair was mussed. He was carrying a wicker tray laden with food and decorated with a vase of flowers.

Uncertain blue eyes lifted to meet questioning brown ones. Elyssa felt her heart skip a beat. Maybe two. She was conscious of a tug of attraction and a tremor of anxiety. It was hard to say which she found more disturbing. Both were indications of weakness, and weakness was something she knew she couldn't afford in this situation.

"Good morning," Alex said quietly. The smile he'd given Sandy had faded. His expression was guarded and there was a hint of stiffness in his stance.

"Good morning," she responded, attempting to match his tone. She hugged the sheet a little closer. Even at a distance, even with her defenses up, Alex's aura of bred-in-the-bone masculinity had a very potent effect on her.

"Come in, come in, Mr. M'ran," Sandy commanded, gesturing with both hands. She hopped backward as Alex stepped into the room, then pirouetted to face her mother. "It's bre'kfist in bed for you, Mommy!" she announced gleefully.

Elyssa knew there was no way she could reject Alex's surefooted approach without dulling the sparkle in her daughter's bright eyes. So, she simply sat still as he moved to the bed in a half dozen lithe strides then leaned over to position the tray across her lap.

His tautly muscled upper arm brushed against her for an instant, and she inhaled sharply as a shudder of response went through her. The clean male scent of his skin filled her nostrils. She eased her grip on the sheet she'd been using like a shield without really thinking about what she was doing.

She saw Alex's eyes flick sideways, then narrow. The arrogant line of his jaw went rigid. After a moment, he straightened up and took a step back from the bed. His hands were balled into fists at his sides.

Something in his manner made Elyssa look down at herself. She flushed with embarrassment as she realized that the strap of her gown had slipped off her right shoulder again. This had caused the bodice of the garment to fall away from her body, baring the tops of both her breasts.

Avoiding Alex's gaze, Elyssa hastily tugged the strap back into place and readjusted the front of the nightgown. She would have pulled the sheet back up around her, too, but Sandy chose that moment to climb up on the bed, trapping most of the linen beneath her body.

"What do you say, Mommy?" the little girl prompted, squirming around until she found a comfortable position.

Elyssa blinked. She didn't have to look at Alex to know he was watching her. The assessing stroke of his eyes was as tangible as a physical touch. It made her whole body tighten. Her stomach knotted.

"Ah—what do I say about what?" she asked distractedly, surveying the tray in front of her. Fresh flowers. Fresh fruit. Fresh rolls. Fresh coffee. A very tempting presentation. Unfortunately she didn't think she could swallow a bite with Alex in the room.

"What do you say to Mr. M'ran for bringing you bre'kfist?" Sandy elaborated, a faint hint of reproof in her tone.

"Sandy, I really don't know what—oh." Elyssa broke off, abruptly realizing that she was being treated to a taste of her own method of teaching manners.

"You're s'posed to say thank you, Mommy," her daughter reminded her severely, shifting her weight. The tray tilted slightly. Elyssa steadied it automatically with one hand. "You always make me say it. No matter what. Like I had to say it to Megan B. Russell at my birthday party even though she gave me the most ugliest T-shirt in the whole world for a present and I didn't even want her to come in the first place."

Something about Sandy's aggrieved tone made Elyssa want to laugh. She suppressed the urge. Glancing up at Alex, she was startled to see that the corners of his sensually shaped mouth were twitching. Their eyes locked for a split second. The knot of tension she'd felt only moments before relaxed. The taut strands of uneasiness melted into fluttering ribbons of warmth.

Elyssa cleared her throat. "Thank you, Mr. Moran," she said softly.

"You're welcome, Ms. Collins," he responded.

"That's right," Sandy approved, picking up a slice of pineapple from her mother's tray. She nibbled on the fruit for a moment or two, then tilted her head and declared, "You should say thank you to me, too, 'cuz it was my idea."

Another laugh tickled the back of Elyssa's throat. "Well, thank you to you, too, in that case," she said obediently.

"I even picked the flowers for your tray," the little girl went on proudly. She paused long enough to finish the pineapple spear. A few drops of juice dribbled down her chin. "Mr. M'ran told me what kind they were. He knows everything." She pointed at the blossoms and recited, "That's booger-millas. That's frangi-pansies. That's ollie-ander. And those pink ones are orchids. I told him I 'specially wanted them 'cuz they're like those ones you got in New York." She looked over her shoulder at Alex. "'Member? I told you she brought them home from work and they made our house smell like a garden."

"I remember," Alex answered.

"Well, actually, Sandy," Elyssa felt compelled to say after a moment, "Mr. Moran was the person who sent me those orchids."

Sandy regarded Alex with something like awe. "Did you send them all the way from here?" she asked. "On an airplane?"

"I'm afraid I sent them from an ordinary flower shop on Fifth Avenue, Sandy," Alex conceded.

Sandy looked disappointed for a second, then gave him a reassuring smile. "Well, they were still really pretty," she acknowledged generously. She helped herself to another slice of fruit from her mother's tray. "Did mommy say thank you for them?"

"Yes, she did."

Sandy nodded her head and made an approving sound through a mouthful of ripe mango.

A few seconds of silence slid by. Elyssa picked up a small silver coffeepot from the tray and carefully poured herself a cup. Taking a sip of the dark, fragrant brew, she searched for a safe topic of conversation. She eventually focused on Sandy's decidedly off-center hairstyle.

"Did you do these by yourself, sweetie?" she asked, reaching forward to gently tweak one of her daughter's pigtails.

Sandy—who had finished with the slice of mango and progressed to a roll—chewed vigorously for a moment, then gulped. "Except for what Mr. M'ran helped me with," she replied.

Elyssa found it impossible not to glance at Alex. He was watching Sandy, an expression of tender wonderment softening the hard angles of his face. Elyssa caught her breath. She understood the emotions he was feeling. She, too, had looked at their daughter and marveled at the idea that she'd had a part in her creation. It was something that inspired both humility and exultation.

Alex seemed to be as sensitive to the touch of her eyes as she was to his. He shifted his gaze suddenly and looked at Elyssa, a hint of embarrassment altering his features. One corner of his mouth kicked up into the start of an uncomfortable smile.

"I'm not exactly an expert when it comes to pigtails," he told her.

"It takes some practice," she acknowledged.

"Mommy's really good at them," Sandy volunteered. She munched down the remainder of the roll she'd been eating, then wiggled around to face Alex. "Did you know she used to have hair even more longer than I do, Mr. M'ran? She showed me a picture once. From when she was in high school. Her hair was all the way down her back, like a princess. She looked really beautiful."

"Sandy—" Elyssa began, putting down her coffee cup. Her memory flashed up the snapshot Alex had shown her a week before. She'd had hair all the way down her back in that picture, too. She felt a tinge of heat stain her cheeks.

"I'm sure she did," Alex said.

"But she looks really beautiful now, too, huh," the little girl went on.

"Sandy—"

"Yes, she does," Alex affirmed, his voice dropping a note or two.

"*Sandy*—"

The little girl twisted around. "What, Mommy?" she asked impatiently, then cocked her head and wrinkled her nose. "How come your face is red?"

Elyssa made an inarticulate sound of dismay. She didn't know what to say or do.

Alex, it seemed, did.

"I think it's time we gave your mother some privacy, young lady," he declared firmly, stepping forward. He plucked the little girl off the bed with the unthinking ease of a man who'd spent years lifting steel and laying stone.

"What's privacy?" Sandy wanted to know, allowing herself to be set on her thong-shod feet.

"It's what grown-ups like when they eat breakfast in bed," Alex answered, flicking one of his daughter's pigtails.

"Oh." Sandy looked at her mother questioningly. "Do you want some of that now, Mommy?"

"Just for a little while," Elyssa replied, managing a smile.

"Well, okay. You have some privacy. Mr. M'ran and me will go to the beach and look out for sharks."

The next five days were among the most unsettling of Elyssa's life. Yet she came to recognize there was a definite pattern to them. It was a complicated pattern, to be sure, full of twists and turns, shadow and light. At its heart was Sandy.

Innocently, artlessly, she drew Elyssa and Alex together, serving as both bond and buffer. She had a knack for smoothing over the strained silences that sometimes fell between them. Elyssa lost track of how many times tensions had flared only to be soothed by shared smiles or laughter.

But Sandy also had a disconcerting talent for creating emotional chaos with casual remarks. When she trusted, she talked about anything and everything. And she obviously trusted both her mother and "Mr. M'ran," because she left almost nothing unsaid in their company. She confided, queried, cajoled, and commented.

Short of clapping a hand across the little girl's mouth, it was impossible to censor her. Elyssa soon concluded that her only options were to try to redirect the course of her daughter's conversation when she could and to pray that Alex wasn't paying attention to Sandy's chatter when she couldn't.

She had, on the whole, more success with the former than the latter. This was because Alex listened to Sandy. He really listened. In fact, he occasionally seemed to be much more interested in her childish chitchat than in anything her mother might have to say.

Not that Elyssa could fault him for that. The attention he showered on their child touched her deeply, especially since she'd begun to understand how closely Alex guarded his emotions.

Of course, she realized that the time Alex devoted to Sandy also gave him answers to questions he couldn't—or wouldn't—put to her. But she wasn't able to object to the situation without being hypocritical. She, herself, was quite willing to listen and learn every time Sandy decided to ask Alex about some aspect of his life.

The pattern began to unravel—or reshape itself—the morning of their sixth full day on Isla de la Corazón. After swearing a long and complicated pledge that he would protect her from sharks, Alex had coaxed Sandy into the translucent aquamarine waters of the sea for a swimming lesson. Elyssa had remained on the beach, relishing the warmth of the sun on her skin and watching father and daughter play together.

It was Alex who was the focus of her attention. He was wearing a nylon swimsuit that met the demands of propriety and not much more. The garment was white, contrasting starkly with his sun-bronzed skin. Its snug fit emphasized his masculinity.

The physical strength that was so much a part of him was very obvious in the golden island light. The sleekly powerful shoulders. The broad, hair-whorled chest, and flat belly. The narrow yet muscled hips and strong, sinewy legs. Every inch of his tall, tanned body spoke of an elemental virility.

Elyssa shifted, the plush nap of the towel she was sitting on stroking the backs of her legs. Picking up a handful of fine white sand, she let it sift slowly through her fingers. She was conscious of a shimmering internal heat that had nothing to do with the sun. She ran her tongue over her lower lip, tasting the faint tang of sea salt.

Is this what I felt the first time I saw him? she asked herself. This...restlessness? Did I have any idea what was going to happen between us?

She'd learned that she and Alex had met on a beach much like this one on the east side of the island. The afternoon after their arrival, he'd taken her and Sandy on a sightseeing tour in the Jeep. From time to time, she'd seen something that had stirred a vague sense of familiarity, but there'd been no shock of recognition, no rush of returning memory. She'd found herself glancing at Alex, knowing her eyes were full of questions. He'd answered some of those questions with small movements of his head and offhand comments about his "other visits" to Corazón.

She'd given him no opportunity to answer the others. That would have required being alone with him. And, although Elyssa knew the private conversation they'd had the night she'd returned to Corazón had been important and necessary, she was wary of what another one-on-one discussion might provoke.

Alex hadn't pressed her, although she was certain he was aware of her acts of evasion and avoidance. Her reaction to this was contradictory to say the least. Sometimes she interpreted his behavior as a matter of kindness and consideration. Other times she wondered if it was the result of a lack of caring.

Her hand closed around another fistful of sand. She didn't know where she stood with Alex. She didn't know where he stood with her, either. God, she didn't really know where she stood with herself at this point! If only she could remember what had—

"Mommy! Mommy!" A dripping wet Sandy flung herself down on the towel spread next to Elyssa. Her breath was coming in and out in quick pants. "Did you see me? I made my face go in the water three times! I even opened up my eyes!"

"Three times?" Elyssa echoed, guiltily aware that she'd missed her daughter's great accomplishment. She reached forward and pushed a sodden lock of hair off Sandy's sungilded cheek. "That's wonderful."

The little girl beamed. "I floated on my back, too," she reported eagerly. "Mr. M'ran held on in case I started drownding."

"I bet you'll be floating on your own in a couple of days."

"I wouldn't be at all surprised," Alex concurred, dropping to his knees next to Sandy in an easy, athletic movement. The little girl turned toward him like a flower turning toward the sun.

"And then you'll teach me dog-paddling, right?"

He nodded. "If you want to try it."

Sandy's response to this was to give him a damp hug. Elyssa watched Alex return the embrace, sensing he was controlling himself very carefully as he did so. His eyes met hers for an instant. She read both pain and pride in them.

Once released, Sandy sat back on her heels, tilting her head to one side. Her brown eyes flicked back and forth several times as she nibbled on her lower lip. Elyssa felt a prickle of uneasiness, realizing the little girl was working herself up to say something.

"Sandy—" she began.

Her daughter didn't respond. Her attention was fixed on the man who'd protected her from sharks and safeguarded her from "drownding."

"Can I call you Uncle Alex?" she asked in a rush. "Please? Instead of Mr. M'ran?"

Elyssa's eyes slewed instantly to Alex. He'd gone very still, his features coalescing into immobility. Oh, God, she thought, sensing what must be going through his head. Oh, God, no. This isn't fair to him.

Alex took a deep breath, then reached forward and brushed a finger along the line of his daughter's nose. "I'm very honored by the idea, Sandy," he told her quietly. "But I don't believe in calling people things they aren't."

Sandy frowned, obviously uncertain of whether this was a definite yes or no. "I call Aunt Nikki Aunt Nikki even though she's not really."

"Sweetie, that's different," Elyssa said quickly.

Sandy looked at her, nose wrinkled, forehead furrowed. "How come?"

"Well, because Alex—I mean, Mr. Moran—"

"You can call me Alex, Sandy," Alex cut in abruptly, putting an end to Elyssa's floundering. "Just plain Alex. If your mother says it's all right."

Sandy's eyes widened. "Alex?" she repeated in a hushed voice. "Alex—like a grown-up?"

Alex nodded. His mouth curved into a smile that didn't touch his eyes. "You're six. That's pretty grown up. But your mother has to give her permission."

"Mommy? Can I? Can I call Alex Alex?"

Elyssa blinked against a sudden prick of tears. She'd told Nikki she'd been certain Alexander Moran wouldn't hurt his daughter and she'd been right. But she'd never really considered the pain he might have to endure to avoid doing so.

"Yes," she answered, "of course you can."

"Where's Sandy?" Alex asked about three hours later, walking out onto the terrace. He'd spent the past twenty minutes on the phone with Philip Lassiter, firmly assuring him that all was going well. He'd been lying through his teeth, and he strongly suspected his friend knew it.

Elyssa sat up. She'd been leaning back against the cushions of the chaise longue, turning the day's events over and over in her mind. She offered Alex a tentative smile.

"She decided to help Luisa make dinner," she replied. Luisa was the plump and pleasant island woman who worked as Alex's housekeeper and cook. She'd captured Sandy's attention the day after their arrival with a demonstration of the fine art of chicken plucking.

"I see."

After a brief hesitation, Elyssa swung her legs off the chaise. She smoothed the brightly patterned skirt of the scoop-necked sundress she'd donned after returning to the villa, then made a small gesture inviting Alex to come and sit next to her.

Alex crossed to the chaise slowly. He stood for a moment, looking down at Elyssa, trying to gauge her mood. While there was a hint of uncertainty in her manner, she met his gaze steadily.

When he finally sat down, it was close enough so that he could smell the sweetly elusive scent of her perfume.

"Alone at last," he remarked after a few seconds.

Elyssa shifted a little, knitting her fingers together. "I suppose I've been pretty obvious," she said awkwardly, referring to her efforts to avoid him.

"I understand."

"Do you?"

"This is a difficult situation for both of us, Elyssa."

She nodded, dropping her eyes. She was very conscious of his nearness. Although he'd changed when he'd come in—putting on jeans and a loose-fitting cotton shirt—she could not obliterate the mental image of how he'd looked standing in the sea clad in nothing but a narrow strip of white nylon.

"I'm sorry about what happened on the beach with Sandy," she said eventually.

"Don't be."

"But—"

"It means something that she wanted to call me Uncle Alex," he interrupted.

Elyssa looked at him, remembering the pain and pride she'd seen in his eyes when he'd hugged their daughter. "I had no idea she was going to ask you if she could."

Alex cocked his head to one side, assessing her with narrowed eyes. "Were you afraid I was going to tell her who I am?"

"No." The answer was quick and unequivocal. "I know I can trust you with her."

He caught his breath at Elyssa's unexpected expression of faith. He'd been very careful with her since the night of her arrival. Now, sensing a change in her attitude, he decided to push . . . just a little.

"But you don't know if you can trust me with you, do you." It wasn't really a question.

She stared at him for a long time. Her response, when it finally came, was edged with frustration.

"I don't know if I can trust *me* with me," she said. Getting to her feet, she crossed to the terrace railing. She looked out toward the sea, which lay glittering beneath the setting sun.

There was a long pause. Alex studied Elyssa silently, trying to make sense of her last response. At the same time, he found himself cataloging the physical changes more than six and a half years had made in her. It was something he'd done before, something he no doubt would do again.

She'd been lovely when he'd first known her. She was lovelier now. It was like comparing a budding flower to a blossoming one. Even in distress, she shimmered with a woman's strength and sensuality.

Alex watched Elyssa raise a hand and brush a lock of pale gold hair back from her face. Her breasts lifted with the movement of her arm, straining against the fabric of her dress. The peaks of her nipples were clearly defined for a moment.

His body tightened as he vividly recalled what he'd seen six days before when he'd leaned over to place the breakfast tray across Elyssa's lap. It clenched on a fierce shaft of need when his mind rolled back eight days further and he remembered stroking aside a pale pink, lace-trimmed slip so he could claim the feminine flesh beneath with lips and fingers.

He sucked in a deep breath, fighting to control the desire that was surging through him. Drawing on every ounce of self-discipline he had, he wrenched his thoughts out of the fiery path they'd been following. He forced himself to go back to what Elyssa had said before she'd gotten up and moved away from him.

I don't know if I can trust me with me.

A strange sentiment from a woman he knew had had no one but herself to rely on under the most trying of circumstances. Elyssa had woken up in a hospital room with a hole in her memory—alone. She'd gone to New York after she'd discovered she was pregnant—alone. She'd borne their daughter alone and raised her in the same way. While the file Philip had turned over to him before he'd left for Corazón had indicated she'd had some money from a modest trust fund set up by her late father, the investigative report had made it clear she'd shouldered the burdens of single motherhood by herself.

So why would she feel she couldn't trust herself? Why would she be so uncertain? What had prompted the confession of insecurity his instincts told him had come from the very center of her being?

Alex frowned, thinking back more than six and a half years. He'd sensed uncertainties and insecurities in the half girl, half woman who'd called herself Dawn, too. That was one of many reasons he'd treated her with so much care.

He suddenly remembered the fragments of information she'd offered him about her relationship with her stepfather during their first dinner together. The kind of rejection she'd hinted at must have left a cruel mark on her nature. But there had to be more. There had to be something—

Alex stood up abruptly, his mind racing. He crossed to Elyssa in three long strides. She turned, meeting his gaze with shadowed eyes.

"Tell me about Lane Edwards," he said.

His low, intense command caught Elyssa by surprise. A tremor ran through her and she searched his face, wondering what had prompted him to bring up the subject of her former fiancé.

"Why?" she asked, her voice less steady than she wanted it to be.

"Because I need to know."

Elyssa flinched. "There are things I need to know, too."

Alex had kept himself from reaching out and touching her for more than six days. He couldn't prevent himself from doing so now. He smoothed his right palm down the length of her left arm, then stroked his fingertips gently against her wrist.

"I understand that, Elyssa," he told her earnestly, withdrawing his hand. One touch. That's all he could permit himself. "There are two weeks of your life you can't remember. But there are years and years of it I never learned about. Despite everything we've been through together, you're still a mystery to me in many ways. I need to know about you."

Elyssa swallowed, her body quivering in response to the brush of Alex's strong, warm hand. He hadn't touched her except by accident since her arrival on Corazón. Until this moment, she had not let herself admit how much she'd wanted him to.

"You had me investigated," she pointed out.

"Information about facts. No explanations about feelings."

"My...feelings...about Lane aren't important anymore."

"You came to Corazón because of those feelings, didn't you?"

She stiffened, hesitated, then told him the truth as she believed it. "I came to Corazón because I was running away."

"From Lane Edwards?"

"From myself."

"From your—" He shook his head. "I don't understand."

Elyssa averted her eyes. She hadn't expected her words to make sense to Alex. She doubted he'd ever run away from anything—or anyone—in his life.

"Elyssa?"

She sighed. "It started before Lane," she said. "A long time before Lane. I told you my father died when I was young."

"When you were eight."

She nodded. "What I didn't tell you was how much I loved him. How much he loved me." She slanted a quick look at him. "I was his little princess. He made me feel so good. So cherished. Everything I did was wonderful and special as far as he was concerned."

"And then he was gone." According to the report he'd been given, Donald Collins had died of a massive heart attack at age forty-five.

"And then he was gone," she agreed, trying to keep her voice even and not succeeding. "And I decided it must be my fault."

"*What?*"

Elyssa shifted to face him. "I decided he died because of something I did. Something wrong or bad," she explained simply. "I didn't know what it was, I only knew I couldn't risk ever doing it again. So I made up my mind to be the best little girl in the world. I was going to be perfect. I was going to please everyone."

Alex caught a glimpse of where her words were leading. "Oh, Elyssa . . . no."

"I did pretty well for awhile," she went on. "Or, at least, I thought I did. But two years after my father died, my mother got married again."

"To Paul Haywood."

She felt a moment of surprise that Alex knew the name, then remembered the investigation he'd had done. "Yes."

"The man you could never please." Alex's throat was tight. The file on Elyssa had made it clear that while her stepfather was an extremely successful businessman, he was also a cold, even callous, individual. Elyssa had been shipped off to boarding school shortly after he'd married her mother.

"That's not quite true," she answered with a trace of bitterness. "He was very pleased when I started dating Lane. He was even more pleased when we got engaged."

Alex hesitated for a moment. Then, unable to stop himself, he asked the question he knew he had no real right to put to her.

"Did you love him?"

"I thought I did."

"But you don't anymore?"

She sighed wearily. "I loved the idea of being loved," she confessed. "I wanted to get married. To be a wife. To have children." Her mouth curved into a smile that tore at Alex's heart. "Lots of children."

"What happened?"

Elyssa had managed to sustain his gaze until this point. Now she averted her eyes. A part of her felt it would be easier to strip herself naked than to go on baring her soul. But she knew she had to continue.

"The night Lane gave me his ring, we made love for the first time," she said, controlling a small shudder. "I was— I'd never been with a man. It wasn't very good between us. It wasn't very good the next time, either. Or the time after that. I didn't know what to do. Lane was used to more experienced women. I . . . I couldn't please him."

"Did he please you?"

She didn't answer him with words. She didn't need to. The blankness of her expression when she swung her eyes back to meet his was very eloquent. Elyssa had received no pleasure from her fiancé. Nor had she expected to. But it apparently had never occurred to her to consider this.

"Lane went off on a two-week business trip," Elyssa resumed after a few seconds, behaving as though she hadn't heard Alex's question. "The day he was due back, I decided to go over to his apartment and surprise him with a welcome home dinner." She drew a shaky breath. "But I was the one who was surprised. You see, Lane had come home a day early and he wasn't alone."

"Oh, no." Alex's instinctive hostility toward the man who had been Elyssa's first lover turned to hatred.

"Oh, yes," she responded with a ragged little laugh. "It was quite a scene. I ended up throwing my engagement ring at Lane. He finished by making it clear what had happened was my fault."

"Your fault? For the love of heaven, Elyssa!"

Elyssa made a helpless gesture. "He was right, Alex. I should have been the one in bed with him. Not some secretary from my stepfather's company. But I didn't have . . . he needed more than I could give."

The urge to pull Elyssa into his arms and show her very explicitly how much she had to give almost undid Alex. He could understand, given everything she'd told him, why she might have believed Lane Edwards' vicious lies in the past. But, dear God, how could she not see their falsity now? Even if she couldn't remember the passion they'd shared on Corazón, she'd experienced the same ecstasy he had the night they'd made love in his apartment. Surely she must realize—

Alex went rigid. *Had* she experienced the same searing, soaring pleasure he had? he asked himself starkly, doubt stabbing at his soul. He'd been certain until this instant that she must have. It had seemed impossible that what he'd felt had been entirely one-sided.

And yet, she'd left him in the wake of that lovemaking. She'd left his arms, left his bed. She'd abandoned him without saying a word.

"Elyssa—" he began rawly.

He got no further.

"Mommy! Alex!" a treble voice called from inside the house.

He heard the slap-slap-slap of rubber-soled sandals against tile. A moment later, Sandy materialized in the doorway that opened onto the terrace.

"Luisa says it's time to eat dinner," the little girl announced gaily. "Come and see what I helped cook!"

Ten

That night, Sandy insisted both "Mommy" and "Alex" tuck her in.

"Will you tell me a story, Alex?" she wheedled as she snuggled down amid the crisp cotton sheets.

"Sandy, it's way past your bedtime," Elyssa countered, stroking fine brown hair back from a smooth, sun-kissed brow. She wondered how long it would be before her daughter stopped using Alex's name every fifteen seconds. Like a pixie with a brand-new spell, Sandy seemed bent on invoking the two syllables at every opportunity.

"Bu-u-u-hh—" the little girl tried to stuff a gigantic yawn back into her mouth. "But, I'm not even tired," she protested.

"You could have fooled me," Alex teased, his eyes moving from daughter to mother and back again. He was sitting on the left side of Sandy's bed, Elyssa was on the right. "I thought you were going to doze off in the middle of that dessert you helped Luisa make."

Sandy giggled. Her eyelids drooped for a moment. "Did you think it tasted good, Alex?"

"I thought it was delicious."

"Then will you tell me a story for a reward?"

"Sandy," Elyssa chided.

"I'm afraid I'm even worse at telling stories than I am at doing pigtails, baby," Alex replied quietly.

"'M not a baby," Sandy disputed automatically. She yawned again. "It can be a real story. Like how you were a hero in the hurricane."

Elyssa's heart missed a beat. She looked across at Alex and saw that he'd stiffened. "What are you talking about, Sandy?"

The little girl yawned a third time. "Luisa told me when we were cooking," she explained. "A long time ago, even before I was borned, there was this really, really big hurricane here. And other places, too, I think. Alex was here when it came." She frowned suddenly, then looked at Alex. "Did you live in this house then?"

He shook his head. "I was here on a business trip. I ended up staying longer than I expected."

Because of Dawn, Elyssa thought.

"Oh." Sandy nodded her understanding. "And then the hurricane came too fast for you to ex-cape, right? Luisa says nobody even believed it was going to land on this island, but it did."

"Hurricanes are hard things to predict, Sandy," Alex told her seriously. "The one you're talking about turned out to be much more powerful than anyone thought it would be."

"But you were brave and saved people from it, huh. You were a hero."

"I helped where I could." Alex brushed the knuckles of one hand gently against the little girl's left cheek.

Sandy turned drowsy brown eyes back to her mother. "Luisa says this hotel fell down because of all the big winds and people were getting squished inside." She yawned for nearly ten seconds. When she started to speak again, her voice was very fuzzy. "But 'cuz Alex...knows how to...make buildings, he figured...mmm...figured out how to rescue...mmmmm..."

The final words of Sandy's dramatic tale dissolved into a long sigh. Her eyelids dropped shut and her mouth went

slack. After a few moments she murmured something un-
intelligible and burrowed her cheek into her pillow.

Elyssa looked at Alex. "Was that when I told you I'd wait
for you?" she questioned in an undertone. "When you went
to help those people?"

He nodded.

"And when you came back . . ." She bit her lip, imagin-
ing him exhausted in body and mind from what must have
been a difficult, even dangerous, ordeal.

He nodded again, then extended his hand to her. "Let's
go for a walk on the beach and talk."

It was a beautifully clear night outside. The moon was
full. It hung in the sky like a polished platinum medal on
midnight blue velvet, bathing everything in an other-
worldly glow. The surface of the sea looked as though it had
been sprinkled with the shards of a thousand shattered mir-
rors.

"I still don't understand why you came to Corazón,"
Alex commented after they'd walked about a hundred yards
down the beach from the villa. He fully intended to discover the truth about what had happened in his apartment
before this conversation was over, but he wanted to approach the matter slowly.

Elyssa stopped in midstep and turned to face him. "I told
you."

He shook his head, the silver strands at his temples
gleaming in the moonlight. "You didn't just walk out of
your ex-fiancé's apartment and get on a plane."

Elyssa shifted her weight. They'd both taken off their
shoes before they'd left the villa. The finely textured sand
was warm against the soles of her feet.

"No, I didn't," she conceded after a moment.

"What happened?"

"Do you really want to hear this?" she asked a little desperately.

"Yes, I do."

She closed her eyes. Taking a deep breath, she let the
words tumble out. "My mother and stepfather were fu-

rious when they found out I'd broken my engagement. My mother was worried about scandal. My stepfather thought I was throwing away my one opportunity to do something with my life. They both wanted me to give Lane a second chance. Especially after he turned up with flowers, apologies, and promises he'd never be unfaithful again." Her mouth twisted. "He was . . . very persuasive."

"You were tempted to take him back."

Elyssa opened her eyes and looked at him. "I was tempted to give in," she corrected bleakly. "Same result, different reason. I still wanted to please everybody. I still wanted to be the best little girl in the world. Then, one day about two-and-a-half weeks after I'd thrown the ring back in his face, I actually heard myself telling Lane I'd think about going out to dinner with him. And I suddenly realized what I was doing and why I was doing it. I also realized I'd probably go on doing it. I mean, I didn't know how to stop. But I wanted to. Only I didn't think I was strong enough to stand up to all of them. So, I ran away."

"Why to Corazón?"

She smiled crookedly. "I'd read an article about it. I thought it sounded like paradise."

It had been paradise, Alex thought. Paradise on earth for both of them. He wanted desperately to believe there was a chance it could be again.

Neither of them spoke for nearly a minute.

"You went back to your mother and step-father . . . afterward," Alex said finally.

"For a while."

"Until you found out you were pregnant."

"Yes."

"You never thought the baby might be Lane's?"

Her chin went up a notch. "No."

"And you never considered . . ." Alex found he couldn't complete the sentence. He saw Elyssa's hands move up to her abdomen and felt a tearing sense of loss. *I would have been there*, he wanted to tell her. *Sweet heaven, I would have been there for you if I'd known!*

"No," Elyssa answered fiercely, then realized she was pressing her palms protectively against the place where she

had carried Sandy. For a moment she was lost in the memory of what it had been like to feel the first stirrings of a new life growing within her. Then she shook her head to clear it and continued, "My mother and stepfather both tried to pressure me into having an abortion, but I wouldn't. *I couldn't.*"

"Despite the fact that you thought you'd gotten pregnant because of a meaningless romp with a man who didn't give a damn about you."

Elyssa didn't flinch from his harsh words. They were an accurate summation of the conclusion she had reached about what must have happened on Corazón. She'd clung tenaciously to that conclusion until Philip Lassiter had revealed how totally wrong it was.

"I wanted my baby," she said simply.

"So you decided to strike out on your own."

"Not before Lane reappeared and told me he'd be willing to help me with my problem."

Alex was startled into saying something crude.

Elyssa gave a humorless laugh. "Actually, Lane's mother is a very nice woman," she observed. "I think she would have been shocked to find out that the only reason her son was ready to forgive my indiscretion was because my stepfather promised him a vice presidency with his company."

Anger stabbed at Alex with an icy blade. "Edwards *told* you that?"

Elyssa took a half step back, shaken by the aura of barely leashed violence she suddenly felt envelope the man she was standing with. She'd seen him show so much gentleness toward Sandy in recent days, she'd almost forgotten how very dangerous Alexander Moran could be.

"No," she said, thankful that her voice was steadier than her pulse. "Lane didn't tell me. My stepfather did."

Alex had seen Elyssa's small retreat and instantly understood the reason for it. He took several deep, cleansing breaths, trying to purge himself of the cold, killing fury he'd felt on her behalf.

"Let's walk some more," he suggested after a few tense moments.

They covered another fifty yards, then came to a halt once again. Elyssa looked around slowly, her eyes tracking from a stand of sea grape trees across the silvery white beach to the wave-ruffled waters of the Caribbean.

Paradise, she thought yearningly. Paradise forgotten.

"Are you *sure* I never came here?" she asked aloud.

The pain that haunted Elyssa was a palpable thing. Alex could see it in her face and body. He could hear it in her voice. He wished he could find some way of helping her to exorcise it, but he couldn't.

"Not with me," he answered. He ran his fingers back through his hair, a combination of frustration and guilt gnawing at his guts. "You still don't remember anything, do you? It's been a week and you still don't remember."

Elyssa shook her head, her fragile features taut. "I keep reaching. Pushing. Trying to break through. I'm blinded by a barrier I can't feel, but I know it's there. I have moments when I think I catch a glimpse, a hint of what happened. Flashes of something..."

"Déjà vu," he said, offering her the same phrase she'd offered him the night she'd arrived. Lord, that now seemed so long ago!

"Yes and no," she responded, gesturing a little wildly. "Because I sometimes get the flashes when I'm in places you say I've never been. And then I feel nothing when I go someplace I should know very well."

"What about before you came back to Corazón?" he asked. "What about the six and a half years when I was looking for you? There was *nothing?*"

For the first time since they'd come out on the beach, Elyssa hesitated. There had been something, of course. The dream. The arousing, erotic dream. But how could she tell Alex about that?

She caught her lower lip between her teeth and veiled her eyes with her lashes. An all-too-familiar mix of desire and shame assailed her. While she no longer had any doubts about the identity of the man in that dream, she still felt strangely alienated from the woman.

"Elyssa?" Alex questioned sharply. His brain raced, trying to make sense of the sudden change in her demeanor. She was hiding something. He was absolutely certain of it. But what? He stiffened as a possibility occurred to him. "What made you decide to call your daughter Alexandra Dawn?"

Elyssa stared at him, thoroughly startled by the inquiry. "I—I don't know," she faltered, realizing with a jolt that she'd never stopped to consider the implications of the pairing of those two names. "I didn't—Alexandra Dawn just seemed right to me. I hadn't settled on any names when I went into labor. The baby wasn't due for two more months. But after she was born...after the first time I saw her in the incubator...I knew. Her name was Alexandra Dawn. Sandy."

"That's all?" Alex brought his hands up to cup her shoulders and felt her tremble at his touch. She turned her face away from him, evading his eyes. He slid his right palm inward, then up the smooth line of her neck. Capturing her chin with his fingers, he gently forced her to meet his gaze. She was still hiding something. "What? What is it, Elyssa?"

"Sometimes...I dream," she admitted, feeling her cheeks flame.

"You dream?" he echoed blankly.

She nodded. "The same dream. Over and over. I—I dream I'm with a man and we're making love."

Alex felt his blood start to heat, his body start to harden. "Am I that man?"

She swallowed convulsively before she replied. "You must be."

" 'Must be'?"

"I don't remember the man's name or face when I wake up. Only—" Elyssa licked her lips "—only the feelings."

Alex closed his eyes, telling himself he hadn't seen the provocative sheen of moisture her tongue had left. "But it's the same man."

"Yes."

"The same feelings."

"Yes."

He opened his eyes. "How long—?"

She sighed shakily, knowing she had to tell him. "The first time the dream came was about four months after

Sandy was born. There...there was a terrible storm. Thunder. Lightning. Heavy rain. Howling winds."

"Like a hurricane."

Elyssa nodded. She could sense Alex's mind ticking over. Inexorably. Implacably. Inevitably. She knew, to the instant, when he reached the bottom-line.

She wasn't certain what she'd expected his reaction to be. But she definitely wasn't prepared to see a tide of color surge up into his face then drain away. She was even less prepared to see his eyes darken with an appalled kind of shock.

"When it storms, you dream," he said, letting go of her.

"Yes."

"There was a storm the night you came to my apartment, Elyssa."

"Yes."

"Then when I—my God, were you *dreaming?*" His voice splintered on the last word.

"I—"

"You were," he asserted, answering his own anguished question. "You *were.* And then you woke up from what you thought was the dream and discovered you'd actually made—" He stared at her with stricken eyes. "You meant them, didn't you? The things you said to me the next morning when I came to your apartment. They were the truth. You didn't know what had happened. Not really. And you didn't know why it had happened, either. But I—I—oh, God, Elyssa!"

"Alex—" Elyssa began, reaching out toward him. The expression on his face stopped her from completing the gesture or the sentence. It seemed to stop her heart for a second or two as well.

There was a long pause. Finally Alex spoke again.

"You were right to leave me," he told her grimly. "After what I did, after what I wanted to go on doing, you were right."

"No." Elyssa had to deny it.

"Yes." His eyes moved over her face slowly, as though he was trying to commit her features to memory. "I think you should go back to the villa now," he said after several long moments.

"Alex—"

"Please, Elyssa," he was as close to begging as he had
ever been. "Go."

In the end, she did.

Alexander Moran charged, tried, and convicted himself
long before the sun started to come up the next morning.
The sentence was a return to the solitary confinement he'd
known for most of his life. No paroles. No pardons. No exchange of prisoners.

Someday, perhaps, Elyssa would be able to forgive him
for what he'd done to her. She was, after all, a very gentle
and generous person.

Alex was neither. And because of this, he knew he would
never be able to forgive himself.

He accepted his punishment. The only other thing required was that he try to make some kind of reparations for
the hurt he had caused.

He knocked on Elyssa's bedroom door shortly after
dawn. He knew she was awake. Her light had been on all
night, and he'd seen her silhouette moving back and forth
on the sheer curtains only a few minutes before.

She answered immediately, as though she'd been waiting
for him. As the door swung inward, he glanced quickly over
his shoulder at the door to the room across the hallway. It
was still closed, just the way he'd left it a few moments before after he'd finished assuring himself that his daughter
was safe and sound and sleeping peacefully.

"Alex!" Elyssa exclaimed softly. For a second she
thought her knees would buckle beneath her. She held on to
the doorknob until the feeling of weakness passed. "I was
worried," she told him.

Gentle and generous, he thought, noting the shadowy
smudges beneath her sky-colored eyes. Although the hours
she'd spent in the sun during the past week had lent a honey-
peach warmth to her skin, her cheeks were very pale. She
was still wearing the gaily patterned sundress she'd had on
the night before. The skirt was rumpled as though she'd lain
down in it.

"I'm all right," he said, keeping his voice low. "May I come in?"

"Oh, yes, please," she agreed immediately. There was a small tremor in her voice as she spoke and another in her hand as she gestured to underscore her consent. She moved back to allow him to enter. "We need to talk."

"I think we've done more than enough of that, Elyssa," he replied, stepping into her bedroom.

His tone sent a shiver of apprehension through her. "No," she denied.

"Yes." He closed the door behind him very carefully.

"Then why did you come?" she asked after a moment, her eyes flicking back and forth. She felt as though she were surveying a fortress. She saw defenses and more defenses, but no way to breach them.

She wanted to breach them. She wanted to reach through the barriers and touch the treasure of Alexander Moran's heavily armored heart. She wanted that more than anything else in the world.

"I came to tell you that you and Sandy are free to go back to New York."

He'd thought it would be impossible for Elyssa to lose any more color from her face. He'd been wrong about that, like so many other things.

"Wh-what?" she faltered.

He repeated what he'd said, then added, "The charter service doesn't fly today, but I'm sure I'll be able to get you out tomorrow."

"We've barely been here a week, Alex. You said two—"

"I said a lot of things. I regret a great many of them."

Elyssa brought her hands together. "You don't want us to stay here anymore?"

"I blackmailed you into returning to Corazón, Elyssa," he reminded her painfully, evading the question she'd asked. His wants didn't matter.

"But—"

"You never would have come back if I hadn't threatened to try to take Sandy away from you. My God, you probably never would have come near me again—"

"I was getting dressed to go back to your apartment, Alex!" Elyssa interrupted fiercely, taking a step forward.

He blinked, looking as though her words made no sense.

"Running away from you after we made love was wrong," she told him urgently. "It was cowardly. I know that. I knew it over a week ago."

"No." He shook his head. "You were right. I'd forced you—"

"*You didn't force me!*" she disputed, her eyes flashing. She drew a shaky breath, then continued in a soft but intense tone, "You didn't force me to make love with you, Alex."

For one moment the burden Alex was struggling to shoulder seemed to lighten. Then it bore down on him with more weight than ever.

"At the very least, I took advantage of you that night in my apartment," he said steadily. "I knew something wasn't right. Deep down in my gut, I knew. But when I said your name and you turned around..." He paused, his body tightening to the point of pain at the memory. "I wanted you so badly that I ignored what I knew."

Elyssa's breath caught at the top of her throat, threatening to choke her. He'd said "Dawn" that night in his apartment. The name he'd invoked over and over had been Dawn. It had been Dawn he'd wanted...not her.

"And I did force you to come back here," he went on. "Your love for Sandy was the only leverage I had to use and I used it."

"Alex—"

"I can't hold you prisoner to my memories, Elyssa. I'm trapped in the past. You need to be free to face the future. So go back to New York. I promise I'll leave you alone. I won't make any claims on you or Sandy. I would like to have some part in my daughter's life, if you'll let me. But I'll never tell her I'm her father. I'm not, really. You're her only parent. You gave birth to her alone. You've raised her by yourself. Still maybe I can build on what I started with her this past week. I can go on being 'Alex.' I give you my word, I won't push for more than that." He paused, blinking rapidly, then forced himself to finish. "You said the other night that you trusted me with Sandy. Can you—do you still feel that way?"

Elyssa nodded once. She couldn't speak. She knew if she opened her lips she'd cry out from the pain of feeling her heart break.

Alex's mouth curved into a smile that was very hard to look at. "Thank you for that."

She nodded again, biting the inside of her cheek.

He reached forward and brushed the tip of one finger down her cheek. "Be glad you don't remember what we had, Elyssa," he said.

Eleven

"Lys?"

"I'm here, Nikki," Elyssa wiped at her eyes with unsteady fingers.

Roughly sixteen hours had passed since Alex had told her she and Sandy were free to leave Corazón. She'd retired to the white and aqua room where she'd spent seven restless nights a short time before. She'd just finished changing into her nightgown and robe when the phone on the small wicker table next to the bed had rung. The caller had turned out to be a very worried Nikki Spears.

"Either we've got one of the worst connections in the world or you're crying," Nikki commented flatly.

Elyssa tried to summon up a laugh. What she produced was more choke than chuckle.

"Well, you know how these island phone systems are," she said after a moment.

"I also know what you sound like when you've been crying. What's happened?"

Elyssa tightened her hold on the telephone receiver. "Nothing."

"Uh-huh, right. I believe that. I also believe I can buy oceanfront property in Idaho."

"Nikki—"

"Look, Lys, I know something's going on. I had lunch with Philip Lassiter today and he said he talked with Alex—"

"*You* had lunch with *Philip Lassiter?*" Elyssa echoed, startled out of her misery.

"Well, we both had to eat," Nikki returned with an edge.

"You've been seeing him?" Elyssa's pursuit of the matter was prompted by more than a strong desire to shift the conversational spotlight off herself. Given the antipathy that had flared between her friend and Alex's at the airport departure lounge the previous weekend, she was genuinely curious about what might be going on.

"No, I haven't been seeing him," Nikki responded, clearly irritated by the suggestion. "For God's sake, the man probably wears boxer shorts! *Starched* boxer shorts. I'll bet he has them ironed, too, by his faithful valet, Jeeves."

Elyssa almost smiled. "He has a faithful valet named Jeeves?"

An exasperated sound came through the line. "I don't know! But he certainly looks like the type who would. I mean, forget being born with a silver spoon. Philip Lassiter obviously came into the world with a monogrammed service for twenty stuck between his well-bred gums. Georgian silver, no doubt. Handed down from generation to generation. But never mind that. There is nothing going on between the two of us. *Nada.* Zip. Zilch. He simply drove me back into the city after you and Sandy flew off to Corazón last weekend. We got stuck in traffic and we ended up talking. Then he called me this morning and asked me to have lunch with him at his club."

"Did you have a nice time?" Elyssa felt a teardrop dribble down her cheek and brushed it away with the back of her free hand.

"Oh, just utterly marvelous, darling," Nikki answered, her sarcasm as evident as her accent was artificial. "I felt like a piece of pumpernickel at a white bread convention. I don't think Philip's fellow club members understand avant-garde Japanese fashion design. He's probably going to get retroactively blackballed for bringing me into the place. But anyway. To get to my point. Philip said he'd spoken to his good friend and client yesterday. He also said Alex swore everything was just peachy keen fine on Isla de la Corazón.

There was a long pause. Elyssa's eyes stung. Her throat tightened.

"A-Alex may have been exaggerating a bit," she conceded reluctantly, her voice faltering as she said Alex's name.

"Philip seemed to think he was shoveling a load of b.s."

There was another long pause.

"Lys?"

Elyssa swallowed hard, knowing the only way she could avoid telling her friend the truth was to hang up the phone. She knew that if she stayed on the line, Nikki would keep poking and probing until she broke down and confided all.

"I think Sandy and I will be coming back to New York tomorrow," she said finally.

The woman on the other end of the line caught her breath. "You 'think'—or know?"

Elyssa plucked at the belt of her bathrobe. She twisted the strip of pink fabric around her fingers, searching for a way to explain without revealing everything.

"Alex wants us to leave Isla de la Corazón," she said at last.

"He *what?*" Nikki's voice went up an octave between words.

"He told me this morning that Sandy and I are free to go home."

"Without him?"

"Yes."

"Oh God, things must be even worse than Philip thought," Nikki said in an appalled tone. "Do you want to leave?"

Elyssa struggled for control. "No," she answered eventually.

"Did you tell Alex that?"

"No."

"Well, why not?"

"I couldn't, Nikki."

"Couldn't? You mean he stuck his fingers in his ears and refused to listen?"

"Of course not."

"Oh, then you must mean you suddenly lost the ability to talk. Or write. Or do a pantomime."

Elyssa flinched at her friend's scathing tone. She hadn't expected this kind of reaction from Nikki. She'd thought the other woman would greet the news of her impending return from Corazón with approval.

"Nikki, you don't understand," she said quietly.

"So explain it to me."

"I can't explain it to myself."

"You'd better learn."

Elyssa shook her head. "I don't know where to begin."

"Try the beginning," her friend advised trenchantly. "You and Sandy arrived on the island last Saturday. Was Alex there to meet you?"

"Yes."

"Great. What happened next?"

After nearly a full minute of hesitation, Elyssa started to recite the events of the past week. At first, the words came slowly. Nikki almost had to pry them out of her. Gradually, however, she started speaking faster and faster. The final part of the tale she had to tell came tumbling out of her in a torrent of anguished truth.

All the time she was talking, she was hearing Alex's voice and seeing his face.

There was an unsettling and unsettled silence once Elyssa finally finished telling her story. Tears were flowing down her face, scalding her skin, dripping off her chin, and trickling down her throat. She dragged the sleeve of her robe over both cheeks, trying to wipe some of the wetness away.

"You love him, don't you," Nikki said finally. Her voice sounded very peculiar. Almost as though she might be crying, too.

Elyssa closed her eyes. "Yes," she whispered, admitting aloud what she hadn't even admitted in her heart until this instant. "Oh, God, yes, Nikki. I do. I love him so much."

"But you're still going to leave Corazón."

"It's what Alex wants."

Nikki's assessment of this statement was unprintable and to the point.

Elyssa's eyes flew open. She couldn't believe what she'd just heard. "Didn't you listen to what I told you, Nikki?"

"Didn't you?" her friend volleyed back instantly. "You love Alexander Moran. And he obviously loves—"

"Dawn," Elyssa finished rawly. "Alex loves *Dawn*."

"For heaven's sake, who do you think Dawn is?"

"I don't know!" It was a cry from the heart.

"Well, then, isn't it about time you figured it out?"

"Nikki—"

"Losing your past because you got hit on the head and developed amnesia is one thing," Nikki said, flattening Elyssa's attempt to speak like a bulldozer might flatten a tin can. "Deliberately letting go of your future is entirely another. The last time I saw you I called you gutsy. Maybe I was wrong. You told me you were willing to face whatever was going to happen on Corazón. Well, I'm sorry, Elyssa, but it doesn't sound like you're willing to face much of anything. It sounds like the only thing you're willing to do is to run away—again."

The next thing Elyssa heard was an abrupt click of disconnection followed by the metallic hum of a dial tone.

Stunned, she slowly brought the telephone receiver down from her ear. She stared at it for several moments, then placed it back in its cradle. Her movements were very careful, very controlled.

You told me you were willing to face whatever was going to happen on Corazón. Well, I'm sorry, Elyssa, but it doesn't sound like you're willing to face much of anything. It sounds like the only thing you're willing to do is to run away—again.

How could she? Elyssa wondered numbly. How could Nikki have said that to me? I was willing to face what happened here. I'm still willing to. And I'm not running away again! Alex is making me go.

Her breath suddenly jammed at the top of her throat. She felt her face go white and she swayed dizzily. Her vision blurred. Her heart started to pound. For a second, Elyssa thought she might faint. Then the wooziness and weakness passed. Her head cleared at though it had been plunged into ice water.

Everything snapped back into focus.

But nothing looked quite the same as it had before.

Dear Lord, Elyssa thought. *What have I been doing? What was I about to do?*

She didn't want to leave Isla de la Corazón, but she'd been prepared to go because Alex had told her to. She'd been ready to revert to her role as the good little girl who did what other people wanted because she was too frightened to do anything else.

Well, dammit, she wasn't a little girl—good or otherwise! She was a grown woman who'd borne a child by the man she loved. *She loved Alexander Moran!* It didn't matter that she couldn't remember what had happened between them in the past. She knew what she wanted to happen between them now, in the present.

And Elyssa knew what she wanted to happen between them in the future, as well.

Alex brushed his fingertips very gently against his daughter's cheek, wondering if this was the last time he'd have a chance to stand by her bedside and watch her sleep. The realization that it probably was ripped at his heart the way a predator rips at its prey, but he forced himself to accept the pain.

His gaze moved over Sandy's face, absorbing every nuance. The downy brows. The almost translucent eyelids with their feathery brown lashes. The freckle-dusted nose. The soft little mouth that curled up at one corner in a secret smile.

There was so much of her mother in her. So much...

Sucking in a shaky breath, Alex withdrew his hand and straightened up.

"Good night, Alexandra Dawn," he whispered huskily, then pivoted on bare feet and moved silently toward the door.

* * *

Wherever Alex was, Elyssa was going to find him. And once she'd found him, she was going to say what needed to be said and do what needed to be done. She was going to face him . . . and herself.

She crossed the tiled floor of her bedroom and flung open the door.

An instant later, she collided with the man she was seeking.

"Elyssa!"

Alex reached out reflexively, catching her by the upper arms in a bid to help her retain her balance. He could feel the warm resilience of her flesh through the fabric of her robe. The headily feminine scent of her filled his nostrils, making his head spin.

"Alex!"

Elyssa brought her hands up in a purely instinctive movement and braced herself against his chest. Alex was shirtless. Her fingers tightened, absorbing the heat of his naked skin and taut strength of the muscles beneath.

For a few breathless seconds they simply stood there in the hall outside their daughter's door. Still. Silent. Eyes locked. Bodies only inches apart.

Alex never knew how he found the strength of will to release Elyssa and take a step back, but he did. "I was checking on Sandy," he said.

"I was coming to find you," she replied.

He shook his head a little, trying to clear it. No, he thought, ruthlessly quelling the brief flare of hope ignited by her words. He couldn't have heard her correctly. And, even if he had, there was no way in the world she could have meant what he wanted her to mean.

Reminding himself of the reality of their situation he said, "I called the charter service—"

"No," Elyssa interrupted, closing the distance he had opened between them. "I don't want to hear about the charter service," she declared. She heard him inhale sharply as she laid her palms against his bare chest once again.

"I don't want to hear about the plane that's supposed to take me away from here," she went on intensely, spreading her fingers wide. She could feel Alex's heart hammering beneath her right hand. Its urgent rhythm matched the wild pounding of her pulse.

"You don't know what you're doing," Alex told her tautly, capturing her wrists. He meant to pull her hands away. Instead he ended up covering them with his own and pressing them even more firmly against his body.

To touch and be touched was both agony and ecstasy for him. He wanted more. He wanted to kiss Elyssa. To caress her. To sweep her up in his arms and carry her off to the center of the bright and burning universe they created when they made love together. But he had no right to act on those wants and he knew it.

With a boldness she would have denied being capable of only minutes before, Elyssa went up on tiptoe and brushed her mouth over Alex's. Once. Twice. Three times.

"Yes, I do," she whispered. She nibbled at his lower lip and felt him stiffen. She licked the spot she'd nipped and felt him shudder.

Alex was on fire. His blood was pulsing though his veins like molten lava, pooling heavily between his thighs. The fit of his jeans went from snug to glove tight. Still, he struggled to control himself.

"Elyssa, please—"

"There's no storm, Alex," she told him throatily, kissing one corner of his mouth and then the other. "This is no dream."

"*Why?*" he asked. If she was doing this because she felt sorry for him or because of some sense of obligation—

Elyssa saw the desperate uncertainty in Alex's eyes and understood the reason for it. She reached down and clasped his hands with hers. Palm to palm. Fingers intertwined.

"This isn't an act of pity," she said fiercely, then slowly raised his hands to her lips. She gave him a smile that set his nervous system sizzling. "I want to make a memory we can both share."

Two weeks before in his apartment, Alex had been the aggressor. Now, for the first time in their relationship—indeed, for the first time in her life—Elyssa took the lead. She drew him out of the hallway and into her room. Ever mindful of the child they had created, she closed and locked the door once they were inside.

Elyssa had left the lights on when she had gone in search of Alex. There was really no need to keep them burning. The moonlight filtering through the sheerly curtained windows would have provided more than enough illumination. Still, she didn't switch the lamps off. She wanted to see him as clearly and completely as she could.

She wanted him to see her in the same way.

I'm here, she'd told him the first night of her return to Isla de la Corazón and she'd meant it.

For a moment they faced each other as they had in the hall. She, willing. He, still a little wary. Both of them wanting so badly they were trembling with it.

And then she moved. He moved, too. The distance between them dwindled and virtually disappeared.

"Elyssa," Alex whispered huskily, gazing down into her upturned face. He found himself drowning in her beautiful blue eyes. They shimmered with a sensuality that was as old as Eve and a certainty that seemed newborn. He slipped his arms around her. "Oh, Elyssa, if you only knew—"

"I do, Alex," she answered. "I finally do."

Again, she laid her palms flat against his body. She slid them slowly upward, relishing the contrasting textures of him. Her fingertips found his nipples amid the rough silk thicket of his chest hair. She felt him go rigid, as though the contact jolted him. She heard him exhale on a shuddery sigh a moment later.

"Oh, Lord," he groaned. Maybe he was the one dreaming this time, he thought. If so, he hoped he would never wake up.

His nipples were tight and hard, yet exquisitely sensitive. They were even more so when she began to move her hands again. By this time, Alex's hands were moving, too, stroking up to her shoulders, then smoothing down to her waist. He wanted to touch her everywhere.

Elyssa's lashes fluttered. Her nostrils flared. There was a claiming quality to his caresses that made her tremble. A tenderness that made her want to weep. She felt her body flowering in response to Alex's cherishing touch.

She took his face between her palms, rubbing the pads of her thumbs against his hard cheeks and going up on tiptoe once again. She touched his mouth with her own. After a few moments, the teasing contact blossomed into a tantalizing kiss. Their lips separated for the space of a swiftly indrawn breath, then caught and clung.

Alex's arms tightened, pulling her close. The living warmth in him called to the loving warmth in her. She arched into his embrace, glorying in the intimate matching of their bodies. She splayed her fingers and worked them deep into his hair.

"Elyssa. Elyssa . . . love," he murmured a little hoarsely. He kissed a path from her lips to her jaw, then nuzzled at her neck. The caress was feather light, but it made her feel as though her skin was being licked by flames. The gentle fan of his breath sent a shiver of pleasure cascading through her.

Soon, however, she wanted to savor the tastes and textures of his mouth once again. She flexed her fingers against his scalp, wordlessly signaling her hunger. Alex turned his head in response.

Their mouths met and mated. Her lips parted. So did his. Her tongue came in sinuous search of his. The kiss deepened and grew more desperate. Their tongues touched. Tangled. Elyssa whimpered, the sound fragmenting in her throat.

She had no memory of his taking her robe off. She only knew that the garment was wrapped about her one moment and puddled on the floor around her ankles the next. Alex ran his palms up and down her arms as though polishing her just-bared skin. After a few seconds, he cupped her breasts with his hands. He feathered his thumbs across her nipples, coaxing them to peak and pout against the thin fabric of her nightgown.

Elyssa slid her hands down Alex's taut, tempered body until she encountered the waistband of his jeans. Blindly, she fumbled for the button that held it closed. She found it.

Undid it. Then she sought the small metal tab that was the key to freeing him for her touch.

A spasm of pleasure so intense it was almost pain wracked Alex as he felt Elyssa take him in her palm. He groaned as she traced the length of his hardness with slow, sultry fingers. From base to tip and back again, she caressed him. He gasped as she cupped the twin weights that balanced the blunt rod of masculine flesh. For one blazing second he thought his self-discipline would yield completely to her delicately deliberate explorations. Somehow, he managed to retain at least a semblance of control over his responses.

The sound that issued from Alex's lips was so close to a cry of agony that Elyssa hesitated, a hint of insecurity surfacing in the pool of her passion.

"Am I h-hurting you?" she faltered, sensing his sudden resistance to her touch.

"You're killing me," he answered thickly. He tried to smile, but he suspected the expression turned out to be little more than a baring of his teeth. "But I'm loving every moment of it. Every...single...moment."

Elyssa did not completely comprehend the elemental truth embedded in this apparently contradictory reply until a few minutes later. By that time his jeans and her nightgown had been discarded and they were stretched out together on the bed.

She was ready, more than ready, for him. But instead of granting them both the release they wanted and needed, Alex chose to slide his hand between her thighs and press his palm against the pale gold delta that marked her as woman. He caressed her with an arousing intimacy that made her want to cry out for the ultimate assuagement. He ravished her soft, swollen flesh with his fingers, sending waves of fiery sensations radiating outward from her feminine core.

Elyssa knew she would die if Alex didn't stop and she tried to tell him so.

She knew she would die if he did stop and she tried to tell him that as well.

"Alex...oh, Alex..." she moaned, arching up against him as he penetrated her slick, petaled flesh with the tip of one finger. "Oh, please. Oh...*please*..."

"Do you want me?" he asked her hoarsely.

"Yes, oh yes," she answered. "Inside me. Deep... deep... inside me."

"Yes," he agreed fiercely, using his hands to ease her legs apart. The effort of holding back had flattened the edges of his angular features. His eyes were almost closed, although Elyssa could see flashes of molten gold beneath through his lashes.

"Do you... do you want me?" she questioned, opening herself to him.

"More than... anything else... in the world."

Elyssa lifted her hands. She tangled her fingers into his hair and pulled his head down.

"Then take me, Alex," she whispered into his ear in a hot, dark voice she wouldn't have recognized as her own an hour before. "Take me so I can take you."

He did.

And she did.

Release, when they finally achieved it, was a storm of mutual rapture... a storm of shared reality.

Elyssa knew she would remember it for the rest of her life.

Dawn woke Alex with rosy fingers. They caressed his face with gentle warmth, rousing him from the profoundest and most peaceful slumber he'd had in more than six and a half years.

He felt a slashing instant of fear when he realized he was in bed by himself. He opened his eyes.

The gauzy curtains that should have veiled the room's floor-to-ceiling windows had been pulled back. This allowed the lambent golden light of the rising sun to pour in. It also allowed Alex to look out.

What he saw when he looked out was Elyssa. She was standing on the beach with her back to the villa. She had her face turned up toward the sun and from time to time, she lifted one hand to brush a strand of cornsilk hair back into place. An early morning breeze molded the pink robe she was wearing to her slender body.

She hadn't left him. She hadn't run away. And she'd obviously wanted him to know both those things if he awoke and found her gone. Hence the open curtains and the spot she had chosen to stand.

Alex got up, donned the jeans he'd stripped off the night before, and went outside to join the woman he loved.

His heart drummed out a peculiar cadence as he approached Elyssa from behind. He found himself preternaturally aware of his surroundings. The changing color of the sky. The creamy swish of the sea lapping against the shore. The silken texture of the sand beneath his bare feet.

Alex came to a stop about two feet away from her. He knew, though he had no idea how, that she was aware of his nearness. He also knew, though again he had no idea how, that she was waiting for him to speak.

"Elyssa," he said.

She turned to face him with a grace that made him wish he had a gift for poetry.

And then Alex saw that she'd been crying.

"Elyssa?" he repeated.

"I remember," she told him simply.

Twelve

It took Alex a few seconds to recover the ability to breathe. Dear God, how many times in the past month had he dreamed of hearing those two words from this woman? he asked himself. But he'd never imagined she'd say them to him with the silvery tracks of undried tears on her face!

"What do you remember?" he asked.

"Everything," she said, gesturing with one hand. "*Paradise.*"

Alex reached out and touched Elyssa's cheek much in the way he had two nights before when he'd told her to be glad she didn't remember what they'd had.

"And that . . . that made you cry?"

Elyssa trembled sweetly at the butterfly brush of his fingertips and offered him a smile more radiant than any sunrise. She'd realized her tears would distress him. That was one reason she'd come out on the beach by herself. She hadn't wanted him to wake up and find her weeping. She knew that men—especially hard men like Alexander Moran—often misunderstood a woman's tears.

"I've been crying because what I remember is so beautiful, Alex," she told him softly. "You. Me. *Us*. The memories are so beautiful I can't find words to describe them."

A shudder of emotion too poignant to be named ran through Alex when he heard the way she inflected the words "us." She said it the way he thought it—as though their pairing was something infinitely precious.

"When did you remember?"

"Just a little while ago. When I woke up."

"Why didn't you wake me, too?" he questioned. "Didn't you want me to share—?"

"Oh, yes!" Elyssa cried, she lifted one hand and pressed her fingers briefly against his lips, damming up the rest of what he was going to ask. "Of course I wanted to share my remembering with you. But I needed a little time to be alone, Alex. To come to terms with everything. To...to come to terms with myself. I didn't leave you. I didn't run away. Please, I don't want you to think—"

"I don't," Alex assured her quickly. "There was a flash, just a split second, when I was afraid you might have. But then I opened my eyes and the first thing I saw was you."

Elyssa felt her mouth curve upward. She was profoundly thankful her strategy had worked. "That's what I hoped."

Alex smiled a bit, too. "I thought as much. Although—" He let the word dangle provocatively.

"Although what?"

"I wish the first thing I'd *felt* when I woke up had been you."

Elyssa flushed and dropped her eyes. Tendrils of heat and yearning began to curl and uncurl in her stomach. She could not help thinking about what would have happened if she'd been beside Alex a few minutes before instead of standing on the beach.

"Do you remember why you told me so little about yourself when we were together on Corazón the first time?" Alex asked after a few moments.

Elyssa inhaled slowly, then raised her eyes to his. "Yes," she replied. That particular memory was the other reason she'd come out onto the beach.

"Was it a matter of not trusting me?"

She shook her head quickly. "No. I think I trusted you from the moment I saw you on the beach on the other side of the island. It was me I didn't trust."

Alex frowned, remembering the exchange they'd had two nights before.

But you don't know if you can trust me with you, do you, he'd said after she'd told him she trusted him with her daughter.

I don't know if I can trust me *with me,* she'd responded, obviously agitated.

"I don't understand, Elyssa."

"I didn't either, until just a little while ago."

He reached forward and took both her hands into his own. "Explain it to me," he asked. "Please."

Elyssa hesitated for a moment, then began.

"I told you that when I ran away to Corazón I was running away from myself," she said steadily. "From Elyssa Collins. From the little girl whose father died because she did something wrong. From the woman who couldn't satisfy the man she was supposed to marry. I didn't think I could bear to be that person anymore."

Alex shifted his weight, beginning to see the pattern. "So you tried to become someone else?"

Elyssa veiled her eyes with her lashes for a few seconds, then looked up at him once again. "In a way," she agreed. "I don't know if I can make you understand what happened to me in those first few moments after we met on the beach." The vividness of her regained memory of those moments lent her voice a touch of huskiness and heat. "You made me feel things I'd never felt before. Things I'd never dreamed of feeling because I'd never known I was capable of them. And what I felt frightened me a little, Alex."

"Frightened you?" Alex's hands tightened around hers and his brow furrowed as he recalled the potency of the emotions he'd experienced at their first meeting.

She nodded. "I couldn't believe *I* was feeling those things any more than I could believe that someone like you might be interested in someone like me. The real me, that is. The Elyssa Collins me. So, I decided there had to be another me."

"Dawn."

"Yes."

"Oh, Elyssa." He raised her hands to his lips and brushed his mouth against her knuckles.

"I knew you'd find out the truth eventually," she went on, quivering in response to his caress. "I was going to tell you. But everything was so beautiful between us. So perfect. I was afraid the truth would ruin it. I was afraid it would ruin . . . us. And I didn't want that, Alex."

Alex inhaled sharply through his nostrils, then exhaled slowly through his mouth.

"I think I was afraid of ruining 'us,' too," he admitted after a few seconds, releasing her hands. "I think that's one of the reasons I didn't ask you many questions. The two of us—" he gestured at their surroundings "—we were in paradise together, Elyssa. I didn't want to risk letting the outside world in."

A frisson of anxiety shivered up Elyssa's spine as she realized Alex had used the past tense when he'd referred to them being together in paradise. She wanted them to share paradise *now*. She forced herself to resume speaking.

"I was going to explain everything the morning after the hurricane," she said. "But you had to go and help those poor people in the collapsed hotel." She closed her eyes. "I remember saying goodbye after you told me I couldn't go with you because the situation was too dangerous. Part of me wanted to beg you to stay, to keep yourself safe. But I knew I couldn't. So I tried to smile and be brave. But all the time I kept thinking 'What if he doesn't come back? What if he gets hurt . . . or worse?'" She opened her eyes and looked at him once again. "I think I would have died if anything had happened to you, Alex."

He shook his head. "No, you wouldn't have, Elyssa. You would have survived. You're strong. Much stronger than you know."

"I don't always feel that way."

His mouth twisted. "Neither do I. When I came back and found you'd disappeared—" He shuddered. Even now, here in the sunlight with her, the memory of it chilled him to the marrow. "God! I almost lost my mind." He paused, eyeing her narrowly. "Do you remember what happened to you?"

"Some of it," Elyssa responded. She was still a little foggy about the details and she had a feeling she always would be. "After you left, I tried to do what I could with the relief effort in the area where we were staying. I wanted to keep busy. To keep my mind off the kind of danger I was afraid you might be in. I worked until after midnight, hoping you'd come back. Finally I was too exhausted to go on, so I slept for a few hours. The next morning I started helping some of the island families salvage what was left of their belongings. I remember I went into a house where the roof was half blown away. I think I heard a cracking sound, like something giving way. Somebody screamed. It might have been me. It might have been someone else trying to warn me to look out. And then . . . nothing."

"Until you woke up in a hospital in Galveston nearly forty-eight hours later with no memory of the previous two weeks of your life."

"Yes."

"Did you ever try to find out what had happened during those two weeks?"

Elyssa moistened her lips. "No. At first, it didn't seem to matter much. And after I found out I was pregnant—" She hesitated, then continued quietly, "Well, you know what I believed."

Alex did, indeed, know. "You were afraid of having that confirmed."

She nodded. "I think fear contributed to my memory loss, too," she said frankly. "I mean, getting hit on the head may have triggered the amnesia. But I think I would have recovered from it a long time ago if I hadn't been afraid to come to terms with what I'd done . . . with the fact that the woman in my dream was me."

"Is that what last night was about?" Alex asked carefully. "Coming to terms?"

Elyssa met his gaze steadily, knowing her heart must be in her eyes. "Last night was about my loving you, Alex," she answered simply. "Loving you here and now and forever."

"After what I've done—" his voice and body were taut "—you can love me?"

Her lips curved into a warm, womanly smile. "After what you've done, how can I not?"

"Oh, God." Alex uttered the words like a prayer of thanksgiving. He encircled Elyssa with his arms, pulling her close, savoring her sweet weight and scented warmth. After a few moments, he bent his head and kissed her long and deep. She parted her lips on a sigh and he slid his tongue into her mouth, exploring the soft, hidden recesses with lingering eroticism.

Elyssa kissed Alex back hungrily. She brought her hands up and locked them behind his neck, clutching at his dark hair. Need suffused her. Desire lapped at her senses like a tide of liquid heat.

They were both shaking by the time the kiss finally ended. They stood silently in the early morning sunshine, wrapped in each other's arms. Elyssa pressed her cheek against Alex's chest.

"I love you," he said, stroking her fair hair with tender, trembling fingers. "I love you so very much."

The intensity of pleasure Elyssa experienced at hearing Alex say this momentarily deprived her of speech. But embedded in this pleasure there was a niggling, gnawing pain. It was a pain she knew she couldn't run away from any longer.

"Elyssa?" Alex questioned, feeling a change in her body. He loosened his hold on her. "What's the matter?"

Elyssa eased away from him a little and turned her face up toward his. "Do you?" she questioned shakily. "Do you love me?"

He gave her the same answer she'd given him only a few minutes before. "How can I not?" he asked.

She shook her head once. "No. I mean, do you love *me*. Or is it Dawn you love, Alex? It was Dawn you spent more than six and a half years searching for. And the night we made love in your apartment, you...you called me Dawn."

Alex caught his breath. Elyssa's uncertainty stung for a moment, then he understood the reasons behind it, and the hurt was replaced by a desire to relieve what he realized must have become her abiding fear. A fear he'd unknowingly helped fuel.

He waited for a moment or two, his eyes gazing steadily into hers. When he finally spoke, his voice was deep and shorn of defenses. He opened his soul to her without reservation.

"I'm still not entirely certain what happened that night at my apartment," he said honestly. "Except—do you remember talking about my just occupying space there?"

Elyssa nodded a bit uneasily. "I asked you where you really lived if that was so."

"That's right. Well, I was on the verge of telling you about Corazón when the buzzer went off on the oven and dinner was ready. But even if I'd told you about it, I wouldn't have answered your question. Because the truth is, the only place I'd been living—really living—was in the past. I wanted to get back what I'd had, what I'd felt, what I'd been, during those ten days in paradise I had with you. And yes, I associated all of that with the name Dawn, because Dawn was the only name I knew."

Alex paused, searching her face, hoping he could make her understand.

"Maybe I was making love to a memory that night in my apartment," he admitted painfully. "And maybe you were making love to a man you only knew from a dream. But last night— God, last night wasn't a matter of memories or dreams. Last night was *real*. I was with the woman I love. The woman I'm going to go on loving. And the woman is you, Elyssa. Only you. Always you."

"Oh...Alex..." Elyssa felt tears well up in her eyes. His passionate declaration filled her heart to the brim and beyond with joy and hope.

He gathered her close. "Shhh. Shhh. Don't cry," he said, cherishing her with gentle caresses. "Please, Elyssa. Don't cry."

"I c-can't help it." Elyssa turned her head and kissed his shoulder. "Sometimes I cry when I'm happy."

Alex nuzzled his lips against her hair. "Does that mean I'm going to have a weepy wife?" he questioned tenderly.

It took Elyssa a second to make sense of what he'd just said. She looked at him with shimmering blue eyes.

"W-wife?" she repeated in a tremulous voice. "You . . . you want to m-marry me?"

He nodded. "And I intend to make you very, very, happy once I do."

"Oh—Alex!" Elyssa threw her arms around him, caught between tears and laughter.

"Is that a yes?"

"Yes! Yes!"

Alex swept Elyssa off her feet, holding her like a groom preparing to carry his bride across a threshold. He dipped his head and brushed her mouth with his.

"Do you remember the picnic we had?" he asked huskily.

"The one where we never got around to dessert?"

"You were dessert, sweetheart. And how about the midnight swim?"

She gave a throaty giggle. "The one where we never got around to bathing suits?"

His smile was very, very male. "Mmm-hmm."

Elyssa traced the line of his upper lip with her index finger. "I remember . . . you had a mustache," she murmured dreamily.

Alex felt himself begin to harden in response to her tantalizing touch. "I'll grow it again," he pledged.

Elyssa rejected the idea with a languid shake of her head and a teasing smile. "No," she breathed. "I like you just the way you are."

They kissed again. It was a slow, savoring kiss. As full of promises as passion. And when it was over, they spoke of the child they had created on the Island of the Heart more than six years and seven months before.

"What will we tell Sandy?" Alex asked.

"The truth, when she's old enough to understand," Elyssa answered. "For now... we'll tell her we love each other and we're going to get married."

Sandy had only two questions.

To Elyssa, very eagerly, "Can I be your flower girl in the wedding with a pretty dress and pink orchids?"

To Alex, a little shyly, "Can I... can I call you Daddy?"

The answer to both questions was yes.

Paradise, Elyssa thought blissfully as her husband-to-be enfolded her and their daughter in a loving embrace.

It was... for all of them.

*   *   *   *   *

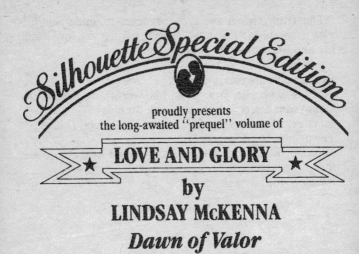

Silhouette Special Edition

proudly presents
the long-awaited ''prequel'' volume of

★ **LOVE AND GLORY** ★

by
LINDSAY McKENNA

Dawn of Valor

In the summer of '89, Silhouette Special Edition premiered three
novels celebrating America's men and women in uniform: LOVE
AND GLORY, by bestselling author Lindsay McKenna. Featured
were the proud Trayherns, a military family as bold and patriotic
as the American flag—three siblings valiantly battling the threat
of dishonor, determined to triumph . . . in love and glory.

Now, discover the roots of the Trayhern brand of courage, as
parents Chase and Rachel relive their earliest heartstopping
experiences of survival and indomitable love, in

Dawn of Valor, Silhouette Special Edition #649.

This February, experience the thrill of LOVE AND GLORY—from
the very beginning!

DV-1

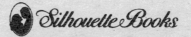

Silhouette Books

Take 4 bestselling love stories FREE

Plus get a FREE surprise gift!

Silhouette romances are now available in stores at these convenient times each month.

Silhouette Desire
Silhouette Romance
These two series will be in stores on the 4th of every month.

Silhouette Intimate Moments
Silhouette Special Edition
New titles for these series will be in stores on the 16th of every month.

We hope this new schedule is convenient for you. With only two trips each month to your local bookseller, you will always be sure not to miss any of your favorite authors!

Happy reading!

Please note there may be slight variations in on-sale dates in your area due to differences in shipping and handling.

COMING IN FEBRUARY FROM

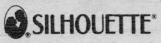

Western Lovers

An exciting new series by Elizabeth Lowell
Three fabulous love stories
Three sexy, tough, tantalizing heroes

In February,	*Man of the Month* Tennessee Blackthorne in *OUTLAW*
In March,	Cash McQueen in *GRANITE MAN*
In April,	Nevada Blackthorne in *WARRIOR*

WESTERN LOVERS—Men as tough and untamed as the land they call home.

Only in *Silhouette Desire!*